PRIOR *of* KAZACHI POST

PRIOR *of* KAZACHI POST

E. M. CLIFFORD

RESOURCE *Publications* · Eugene, Oregon

PRIOR OF KAZACHI POST

Resource Publications
An Imprint of Wipf and Stock Publishers
199 W. 8th Ave., Suite 3
Eugene, OR 97401

www.wipfandstock.com

PAPERBACK ISBN: 979-8-3852-0239-3
HARDCOVER ISBN: 979-8-3852-0240-9
EBOOK ISBN: 979-8-3852-0241-6

01/03/24

Cover Images: Porträtt av en ung kvinna, Björkström, ca. 1915 (adapted)

Children at Kazachi Post, before the Saint Arsenius church. Image courtesy of the Near East Relief Historical Society, Near East Foundation collection, Rockefeller Archive Center

For one to whom there is no greater honor than to serve others

Thus says the LORD of hosts:
Render true judgments
Show kindness and mercy to one another
Do not oppress the widow, the orphan,
the alien, or the poor
And do not devise evil in your hearts against one another

ZECHARIAH 7:8–10

PREFACE

THE guns of August 1914 brought not only war to Europe, but chaos and immeasurable suffering to the Near East. Eastern Anatolia, home to millions of Armenians, turned into a vast killing field, as the Ottoman Empire pursued a policy of ethnic cleansing to rid itself of minority populations within its territories.

A million or more Armenians were expelled from their Anatolian homeland. Many were deported south, through the desert into Syria, while others escaped to the east, pouring into the remote corner of the former Russian Empire known as the Transcaucasus.

Beginning in 1915, terrible reports of violence and deportations began to reach certain persons in the West. One of these individuals was Henry Morgenthau, the American Ambassador to Turkey. Alarmed, he began to collect information about the fate of Armenian and Assyrian Christians in Anatolia, and then to contact those in the United States who were in a position to respond.

Among these were James Barton, himself a former missionary to Turkey who later served as Foreign Secretary of the American Board of Commissioners for Foreign Missions, and Cleveland H. Dodge, magnate of the Phelps Dodge mining conglomerate based in New York. In September 1915, they formed what they called the Armenian Relief Committee, hoping to raise funds to alleviate the hunger and homelessness devastating that population.

The financial power and social connections of those undertaking this effort led to the involvement of many of the most influential men of their time: Woodrow Wilson, Charles R. Crane, Samuel T. Dutton, Stuart Dodge, Stanley White, Charles S. MacFarland, John R. Mott, George Plimpton, and many others. These men had ready access to the highest levels of industry and government in the United States, and they leveraged that access into the formation of a new kind of humanitarian enterprise, comparable to modern civil society or non-governmental aid organizations. Their project was incorporated by Congress in 1919 as the Near East Relief, serving displaced Armenian, Assyrian, Turkish, and Arab populations. Its efforts expanded in 1922 to include the Greeks driven from western Turkey into refugee camps upon the destruction of Smyrna.

Though it provided some acute general relief for adult populations, the primary mission of the organization was to create havens for the countless children orphaned and separated throughout the region. This necessitated a commitment not just to feeding and housing, but to raising and educating these children for years as they grew up, until they reached the point of self-support. In all, the N.E.R. rescued over 130,000 orphans during the years 1915–30, and saved the lives of about one million refugees and victims of war through general relief. By 1923, there were 30,000 children living in Near East Relief orphanages in the Caucasus alone.

The N.E.R. raised over $90 million in charitable contributions, plus another $25 million in appropriations and gifts in kind. They developed a masterful public relations campaign to involve givers of every income level throughout the United States. And they engineered the first partnerships of charity with the newly-emerging agribusiness colossus of the Midwest to feed the starving and to market products such as corn and corn syrup to the American consumer.

Hundreds of citizens volunteered to serve; thirty staff members gave their lives, due to accidents, illness, or acts of violence.

The details in this novel have emerged from numerous very revealing primary sources: first-person accounts from relief workers and those they came to help, official audited reports of the Near East Relief organization to the U.S. Congress, contemporary press reporting, and various documents or manuals circulating at the time. In addition, the work of scholars studying and interpreting these events has been immensely valuable. Some of the books, articles, dissertations, and edited materials of great interest are noted in the "Selected Sources."

The characters are based directly upon persons who were actually involved in the effort to rescue the children of a nation. Some—Ernest Yarrow, John Elder, Aram Manougian, F.W. Smith, Leonard Hartill, Haroutioun Der Ghazarian (known as "Dr. Artine"), and others—appear in the book as themselves, while others are adapted for narrative reasons.

The sequence of events, the precise geography of the region, and the physical layout of the orphanage complex at Alexandropol have at times been modified slightly, to aid in comprehension. Also, I have not followed a formal transliteration scheme for the words and phrases in Armenian, instead composing phonetic approximations that seemed plausible to my untrained ear. I apologize for any inaccuracies in portraying the Armenian language or cultural heritage.

The story of the Near East Relief is perhaps the most compelling example of truly altruistic American involvement with the world in the twentieth century. Yet today's public knows next to nothing about it. Perhaps through Penelope Prior the reader will experience a link with these extraordinary events.

NOVEMBER 1918—DECEMBER 1920

Chapter 1

"**B**ut of course, the missionary family must always create a home that serves as a model of good management and taste, particularly when the missionary comes from a class of society that *should* have such a home. One must be aware of serving as an example at all times. That is the chief role of women in the mission field, and this influence is very great, with a civilizing and converting power."

"Indeed. How are they to aspire to a level they have never seen?"

"So, there is a heavy responsibility to entertain regularly, despite the burden. A visit to the missionary's home for these people is like a day spent visiting galleries and museums."

A murmur of approval from the ladies gathered in Wellandette Prior's parlor.

"One must teach one's servants how to receive company. An unmannerly servant may undo one's own warm welcome. And oh dear, how slow some of them are to learn! They want to keep the best room always closed and the curtains drawn. But only if one honors the guest can one impress them, as well. While keeping enough distance to dignify oneself as a foreigner."

"Naturally," said Mrs. Blair.

The ladies in the parlor had come for afternoon tea, and to learn about authentic missionary experiences from their pastor's wife. Wellandette Prior had lived with her family in Tabriz, then the largest city in Iran, for twelve years. Her husband Gordon Prior had been the printer and bookbinder for the American Mission there, producing the Bibles, service books and classroom textbooks in Armenian and Azeri Turkish needed by the mission churches and schools in northern Iran. He was also an ordained clergyman, but his colleagues in the American Mission soon discovered that he had an uncanny knack for alienating Persian believers, so it was thought expeditious to direct his talents toward printing and publishing.

Reverend Prior was now the pastor of the Collegiate Presbyterian Church in Oberlin, Ohio. He and his family had fled Tabriz in 1914, when war broke out between Ottoman Turkey and Tsarist Russia, and consular officials recommended that all European and American residents should leave. It was clear that northern Iran would become a battleground for these great powers.

The Priors and their five children, all born in Iran, departed from Tabriz in their carriage with only a little hand luggage, leaving their exemplary missionary home and all of its contents behind. They traveled with difficulty to Tiflis, then Trebizond, then by boat to Constantinople, arguing all the while with anyone who tried to stand in their way.

"If you wish to make any progress among the people, you must command their respect," Wellandette Prior was saying. "Our furnishings, our manners, our habits and behavior, our dress . . . even a fine leather Bible with gilt edges, prominently displayed in the home," she added, gesturing toward exactly such a prop lying upon an end table in the parlor, beside a lamp with a silken fringe and a glass globe. "Such a setting has itself preached a little sermon. I remember one elderly lady who remarked on the order and beauty of our house. I said to her, 'Sister, recall that Heaven is far more beautiful than this, with streets of gold and gates of pearl. But as no unclean thing enters there, you must have a clean heart and a clean life.' I trust she went away properly stricken with her own sinful state."

"I should hope so, too," said Mrs. Howell.

"And it was so very gratifying to see the Oriental girls trying to imitate our ways," observed Wellandette. "One might find them learning to press flowers, or paint with watercolors. Not well, mind you, but it was a start." All of the ladies chuckled lightly at this remark.

During this entire conversation, the Priors' daughter Penelope was moving silently among the ladies, distributing tea and tiny sandwiches, and steaming like a kettle.

Penny hated it when her mother lectured about Iran to a roomful of credulous ladies, who had no idea that what she was saying was a lot of pernicious poppycock. Penny herself, born in Tabriz, loved Persia with her whole heart, and thought of the Armenian community with whom she grew up as the true home of her sensitive soul.

Penny was now sixteen, a recent graduate of Oberlin High School. Since the Prior family had settled in Ohio when she was eleven, Penny had been pressed into service to compensate for the domestic help they also left behind in Tabriz. And because Wellandette had employed there an Armenian cook, kitchen helpers, cleaning maids, day and night child care staff, a gardener, handyman, sewing girl, laundress, stablehand, porter, and occasional heavy work crews and laborers, that expectation was a heavy one.

She had served her family like a Cinderella for far too long, and raised her own younger sister and three brothers, the way her Armenian nurses and nannies had raised her.

"But my dear Mrs. Prior," asked Mrs. Blair, "How did you ever manage to establish and maintain such a home, in the midst of a heathen wilderness, so to speak? I can scarcely imagine how it could be done."

"We needed the proper equipment, certainly," Wellandette replied. "Everything of consequence must be shipped from home. And we were able to lease a rather nice villa in the European section of town. That kind of house, with the addition of our own American furniture and fittings, almost made us forget that we were there in the interior of Persia."

Penny swallowed hard and went out to the kitchen for a fresh pot of tea.

"How sad that you were forced to leave your household things behind when you left," said Mrs. Howell.

"Gracious me, in wartime one must be ready for every eventuality. Though I do often sigh over our beautiful things, all stolen and despoiled now, I expect. Our fine furniture and books, our paintings, our piano. My mother's silver flatware, our wedding china. Did I ever tell you the story of the wedding china?"

Nooooo, thought Penny desperately. *Please, noooo. Not the wedding china again!*

"I don't think so, my dear. Pray continue."

"Well, when we sailed for Persia on our first voyage in 1902, our crates and trunks were all perfectly packed in cloth and straw, and well stowed, to protect everything. Mr. Prior saw to that! But upon disembarking in Batoum, every item must be unpacked by the customs inspectors. Just looking for bribes, you know. Mr. Prior wasn't about to give those rascals a single ruble to line their pockets. He wouldn't be a party to their corruption—no, not our Mr. Prior!"

Penny was pouring the fresh tea with trembling hands.

"So, in retaliation, the ruffians pulled out every piece of china, un-wrapped it, and tossed away the padding and straw, just stacking the whole Rutherford bone-china table service back into the crates and nailing on the lids. The crates were sent by train from Batoum to Tabriz, and by the time they arrived, all of them were in fragments! Except for one china platter! I saved that one surviving platter and hung it upon the wall of the sitting room like a family portrait."

The ladies all smiled and nodded at one another, and shook their heads in sympathy.

"From then on we had to use our second-best china. But it was a moral victory nevertheless!"

Penny knew for a fact that this story was false. Her mother knew that Penny knew the story was false. Something similar had happened, but not to them. Another family had lost their china in a mishap like this. But Mrs. Prior felt it reflected well on them and their inflexible rectitude, and the noble sacrifices they had made on the mission field; it also indicted the indigenous people as corrupt and careless, which suited her, too. So she had adopted it as her own. And the presence of someone who knew better was not going to stop her.

Penny filled a cup with fresh hot tea and brought it to her mother. But holding the teacup directly above her mother's lap, she let it slip out of her hands.

There was a shriek as the scalding tea drenched Mrs. Prior's lavender silk skirt. The corps of ladies suddenly mobilized with exclamations of concern, ineffectual gestures, and much bustling about with serviettes. Mrs. Prior reassured them that she was unhurt, with a rigid smile on her face.

Expressionless, Penny turned toward the front door. She wrenched it open and hurried outside, without a hat or a coat, leaving the door standing wide open behind her.

"Such an unfortunate accident, my dear lady! So terribly sorry!"

"Never mind, never mind. I'm quite all right. It will dry off in a moment, no harm done," Welly said. Again she failed to speak the truth, as anyone could see that the skirt was thoroughly wet and probably ruined.

The tea party came to an end shortly thereafter. Mrs. Blair and Mrs. Howell left together, and as soon as they were out of earshot, began discussing the incident with relish.

"Poor Mrs. Prior, she does have a cross to bear with that child."

"They say, you know," Mrs. Blair offered, "They say that she's not quite right in the head. The child, I mean."

"Do they, now?" murmured Mrs. Howell, with barely concealed satisfaction.

Penny walked very quickly down Mumford Street and toward the watershed, where the edge of town merged with the forest. A few people who saw her go by noticed her fixed stare and underdressed condition, but they chose not to interfere.

She continued walking until she was well into the forest, surrounded by filtered light passing through leafless trees.

This was Penny's retreat, where she went when the emotional pressure of life in her home was too much for her. She escaped in other ways as well, doing everything possible to get out of the house.

She taught lessons to the children of the Waldorf family, whose son was of very delicate health and unable to attend the local school; to protect him from catching anything dangerous from the other young children, the Waldorfs hired Penelope Prior to tutor the little boy and his sister at home. She also taught a sewing and dressmaking class at the Collegiate Church, part of the organized Clover Society club for young girls. Penny was an accomplished seamstress and had taught a number of the girls to handle a needle.

And she went out into the woods to pray. Out there, she thought no one was likely to see her or hear her. She had perfected a kind of passionate whisper in which she could pour forth her frustration, her lips moving inaudibly, breathing hard, sometimes in tears.

She spent hours in the forest in all kinds of weather, telling the Lord about her selfish whiny mother and her distant tiresome father, her loneliness, her lack of female friends of her own age, the complete absence of any kind of beau or sweetheart in the known universe, the empty horizon of her future, devoid of an interest or objective in life beyond her services to others.

Penny was theoretically ready to begin study at Oberlin College in the fall; she was a good student and assured of admission. But without a professional or even a personal aim, she could not focus herself to do it. So she spent much of her time fretting and chewing on herself, alone.

It was partly these prolonged prayer vigils in the woods that had gained her a reputation for peculiarity, of being "not quite right in the head." It did cause some people to avoid her. Adolescence in isolation can be a very painful thing.

Oh Lord, you know my mother was lying again, she whispered. *How can she be so shameless? She does it just to impress those silly old women. She lies in front of me, as if I don't exist. As if to her I do not matter at all. Lord, why don't you stop her? Like the evil sister in the Blue Fairy Book, make the lying words come out of her mouth like snakes or toads, so that everyone will know what she is doing.*

The light slanting down through the trees moved lower, and the shadows deepened.

Father God, you must help me find a way forward. I can't see what you want me to do. I feel like I am trapped in a small room and someone is slowly sucking out all the air. I confess, it was wrong of me to spill the tea into Mother's lap. I ask you to forgive me. Please, give me patience, make me a better person. I am not worthy of your help, I know that. But I need you so much. Please open the door of this stifling little room and fill my heart with something. Something better than this.

She realized finally that it was evening; she had missed supper at home. The woods were growing dark, the autumn light fading quickly.

It was a Wednesday, and she knew that the Beacon of Providence Church down near the railroad station would be filling up at about that time. It was a rather long walk in the chill of evening without a coat and hat, but she set out for Station Street just the same.

The Lord had visited the town of Oberlin back in the days of Charles Grandison Finney, the famed revival preacher, who became President of Oberlin College in 1851. He was another passionate soul who went out into the woods to seek God—though Penny was not aware of this. He experienced the power of God moving through him "in waves of liquid love," and he rushed to convict his hearers of their need to overcome the stolid formality of traditional Reformed worship and pour out their souls in prayer. He urged that everyone—not only the "elect"—could seize the salvation offered to them and become transformed and alive in Christ.

At Oberlin, Finney stoked a furnace of radical spiritual and social engagement, preaching the power of full commitment to God and to hastening the coming of God's Kingdom. Finney encouraged women to pray aloud in mixed meetings, and insisted that black students and women be admitted to the College. The whole campus became active in the abolitionist movement and the Underground Railroad, facilitating the escape of enslaved persons to freedom. They leapt headlong into the temperance movement, Sabbath keeping, emotional testimonies of conversion in home prayer meetings, and other evidences of a regenerate Christian life.

By the turn of the century, however, the climate of Oberlin perfectionism had cooled. The Collegiate Presbyterian Church, where the Reverend Gordon Prior preached, was as sober and conventional as a big-steeple church could be.

But in other parts of town, the embers of spiritual revival glowed. The Beacon of Providence was the place to seek divine healing and Holy Ghost baptism in the town of Oberlin. Penny found herself irresistibly drawn there. She had been attending their Wednesday evening meetings for more than a year, over the explicit objections of her parents. One could easily infer that their disapproval made it even more attractive.

When she got to Beacon of Providence, things were only warming up. People were arriving directly from their jobs, especially the black employees of the railroad and train station. Porters, janitors, ticket collectors, and food servers made up the core of the congregation. White working-class people joined them, for some reason mostly men. Their voices were raised, filling the small church with the sound and rhythm of their singing: "Ohhhhh Jo-o-nah, go down to Nineveh and serve the Lord . . . " The song leader blended this smoothly into the next song. "I thank God, I know I got religion . . . Jesus done freed my soul . . . "

Penny stood quietly, eyes closed, hands lifted. She allowed the music to flow over and around her, sometimes whispering silently. Everyone knew her there, and they accepted her desire to immerse herself in worship in her own way.

When the preaching started, the people sat down, but their participation continued. There were bursts of praise and prayer all around her. In addition, she began to hear the syllables of speaking in tongues—not hysterical, but low-pitched, melodious sounds, repetitive, even soothing. Penny had never been granted this or any other overt sign of a Holy Ghost baptism. But she listened to it receptively, as just another part of the experience.

The service often went on until late, especially if there were individual testimonies being shared, or people coming forward to drop to their knees, being prayed over by others, with a laying-on of hands. Penny had absorbed enough by that time and decided that she had better go home before someone locked the kitchen door for the night.

She faced a long walk back to the better part of town where the Prior house stood; it was mid-November and the cold passed right through her indoor clothing. But Penny was never very mindful of the weather and barely reacted to it.

She slipped unnoticed into the house and went directly to bed, undressing in the dark, in the room she shared with her younger sister Matilda. She crept under the covers, trying not to disturb her. Matilda, warm and groggy, reached over and took Penny's hand, squeezing it gently as she went back to sleep.

In the morning, Penelope had to go and present herself to her mother, apologizing for the tea incident in abject terms. Her mother received this apology with a stiff nod of the head and a prolonged, calculated, disappointed sigh.

Only a few days later, Gordon Prior arrived home in the evening with a handful of mail and a preoccupied air. The family ate their supper together in the dining room as they normally did. But Reverend Prior still seemed unusually thoughtful, as though something were bothering him.

While the girls cleared the table, he said to his wife, "Wellandette, when you have a free moment, would you please join me in the study?"

"Of course, dear," she replied.

Penelope and her sister Matilda were still in the room. They looked at each other. As soon as they had finished their suppertime chores, the two of them met at a grate in the floor of the upstairs guest room, where an air passage connected with the study below. They could just hear the voices of their parents by lying on the floor with their ears to the grate. They had learned to be absolutely still and listen.

The Priors shared the news of their day, and discussed the latest developments in Europe, where the Armistice had at last been signed putting a formal end to the Great War. It had been an inevitable outcome for some time, and in fact the Armistice of Mudros between the Allies and the Ottoman Empire had already been signed in October.

"That means, you know, that the era of reconstruction is now upon us," Mr. Prior said. "Europe is hard hit, their resources exhausted. But the much more extreme need is in the East, where Turkey has hounded and murdered and deported thousands upon thousands of Armenians and other Christians. My understanding is that they have poured into the Caucasus from eastern Anatolia and northern Persia—helpless refugees with neither a brick nor a stitch among them."

"If some accounts are to be believed, they are actually starving."

"Yes, dreadful reports are emerging, to be sure."

"We were wise to get out of Persia when we did."

"Well, yes . . . it spared *us* a great deal," Gordon said. "But it also meant that we were not there to help when needed, as were the missionaries who chose to stay."

"Like my sister Annalisa? She was mad to stay there, obviously. To sacrifice herself for those native children—it was simply beyond all reason. Of course there are appropriate limits."

"Your sister Nan is not a limited sort of person."

"Indeed she is not. It was always impossible to make her acknowledge the dictates of common sense."

"Be that as it may, those who stayed were in a position to save many lives, as relief funds could be channeled through them to displaced people. They served nobly in many cases, at great cost to themselves. And now it is someone else's turn."

"What do you mean by that, Gordon?" his wife asked. She did not like the direction this conversation was taking.

"I have here a letter from Dr. James Barton, the Mission Secretary. He is now heading up the American Committee for Relief in the Near East. Also known as the Near East Relief."

"I've heard of it."

"This is what you might call . . . a recruitment letter. They are sending survey teams already to assess the needs of people in eastern Anatolia and the Caucasus. Once they have received updated information, they will be able to formulate specific plans to deploy relief supplies and services where they are needed most."

"A . . . recruitment letter?"

"Yes . . . Dr. Barton is aware that we served in Tabriz with the Armenian community there. I have the kind of language skills and experience that they will need to rebuild Armenia."

The two girls upstairs raised their heads and gaped at each other. Some uncomfortable moments ticked away.

"Gordon Prior," said Welly with the sharpest edge to her voice. "Think what you are saying. I have no desire to abandon our home here and go off to save the world. Not now, not ever."

"But that is the missionary's call, is it not? To save the world? At the very least, this is an opportunity to help to save an entire people. The

Armenian race has been persecuted to the point of despair, no more than a step away from utter ruin. Not to mention the Assyrian Christians of Persia. Without our help they are sure to perish."

"I'm quite sure that there are other people who are ready to step up and carry bread to the starving masses. There is no reason why *we* have to do that."

"It's not just a matter of bread, Wellandette," Gordon said sternly. "It's the orphans. The *orphans*. We can't just distribute relief supplies to families. Many thousands of children have no families anymore. They are collecting throngs of children with no known living relatives. Someone will need to care for them for many years to come. They need food and such, but they also need a place to live, with adequate care and education. Many of them have already gone for two or three years without schooling—it's urgently needed. The society's future depends upon rescuing not only their bodies, but their minds."

Mrs. Prior was shaking her head emphatically.

"They want us to produce textbooks and educational materials to establish schools in the orphanages. I think we could adapt the printing process I used in Tabriz for the Armenian-speaking Christian schools there. Only the most basic books at first, and then perhaps more advanced ones."

"Oh Gordon, it's simply out of the question. I won't do it."

"One's personal preference is not the chief concern at a moment like this. The Christian world must respond to this need in order to be able to look at itself in the mirror. We must do our duty, for the sake of the Church itself. A Christian example must be set. Our credibility and self-respect is at stake."

"Yours is, perhaps," she said acidly. There was another long pause as the girls upstairs could almost hear them glaring at one another.

"You made us leave Persia when we had the chance to achieve something great. Something worthy," he said. "I don't want that to happen again."

"You made us go out to a heathen land to live in hardship and privation, thousands of miles from home. I don't want *that* to happen again."

"Hardship and privation? I don't think you know what you are talking about."

His wife made a scornful noise that could not be expressed in words.

"Mrs. Prior, I have made my decision. I want you to know that I shall accept this request from Dr. Barton."

"Well then, Mr. Prior, I want you to know that I shall *not*."

Stalemate.

In the long prickly silence that followed, the girls upstairs held their breath. They *had* to hear what was coming next.

The wheels inside Welly's head were spinning rapidly. She knew very well that, as the head of their household, Gordon had the legal right to compel her to take their family off to Armenia if he chose to. She searched her mind for a way to prevent this.

Then . . . a little beam of inspiration.

"Gordon, my dear, let us be reasonable," she began, using her most ingratiating manner. "I understand your commendable impulse, and it does you much honor. But we must consider the welfare of our own children. James is in high school now and ready to chart his professional future. Maxwell is ten, and Wallace will soon be eight. How on earth would they get an adequate education, if we were to take them away to starving Armenia?"

The girls could not fail to notice that their mother had not mentioned them at all.

"Certainly they must stay here in Oberlin, where they are doing well," she said. "And of course, they need their mother." Penny nearly snorted at this, since Penny had been the one caring for her siblings on a daily basis for several years.

"But it would be a good thing for you to have some stable home companionship for as long as you happen to be abroad," Welly continued. "Someone to look after your needs. Let me make a suggestion. Take Penelope with you."

This statement struck like a bolt of lightning upstairs in the guest room. The two girls gasped and then clapped their hands over their mouths. Fortunately this sound went unheard downstairs in the study.

"Penelope?" said Mr. Prior, in a wondering tone.

"Why of course, dear. She speaks the Armenian language like a native. Surely that would be useful. She keeps house adequately, teaches children their school lessons, and she can sew, knit, embroider and so on, like an expert. She could look after you and perhaps also make a contribution to the relief effort . . . teach the little orphans to knit or something."

Gordon Prior sat quietly, entertaining this novel proposal.

"It might also be very good for Penelope, you know," Welly went on, still speaking persuasively. "That girl is at loose ends. She doesn't seem to know what to do with herself. Her behavior is becoming . . . somewhat strange. Perhaps she needs a challenge such as this to . . . to straighten up and fly right, as it were. And it would get her away from the bad influence of that church down by the tracks. I don't like her mixing with all of those lower-class people."

Gordon frowned, but not in disagreement. He was thinking intently. "That is a most interesting suggestion . . . I will consider this," he said.

"Yes, dear. Whatever you think is best," said his wife sweetly, knowing that the battle was won.

Upstairs, the sisters rushed into their bedroom and closed the door.

"Pen!! Ohhhh Penny, you get to go back there again!" cried Matilda, trying to keep her voice hushed.

Penelope hugged her sister, her face pink with happiness. "I can't believe it!" she exclaimed. "Oh, it's wonderful! To live with the people again, helping as much as I can. I never thought it could happen!" For her, *the people* meant those with whom she had spent her happy childhood in Tabriz.

"I do wish I could come too," said Matilda.

Penny stopped her rejoicing and took her sister by the hands. "What is wrong with me, thinking only of myself?" she said. "Tildy, you know what will happen if I leave. You will have to be the nanny and the house servant in my place. She will treat you the way she has treated me."

Matilda was a strong and steady girl, now thirteen, and she seemed unfazed by this prospect.

"You have done so much for us," she said. "It's time you had a life of your own, isn't it? So it's my turn to carry on. I think I am equal to it."

"Thank you," sighed Penny, embracing her again. "Thank you, Tildy. Let it be as you have said," she added with a smile, using an expression the two girls employed privately, mocking the imperious demands of their mother upon them.

The hard part was when Mr. Prior laboriously laid this whole plan before her, and Penelope had to pretend that she was hearing it all for the first time. And then she had to conceal what her father would consider to be her unseemly excitement at the possibility of leaving home. With what she hoped looked like humble obedience, she accepted the idea. And then began the complicated process of turning it into fact.

The first step was for Gordon Prior to respond to James Barton's letter, laying out his thoughts, and offering the services of himself and his daughter to the Near East Relief. In due course he received a reply, inviting them to make a formal application to the N.E.R. offices in New York. Two lengthy application forms were included.

The reply explained that applications would be acted upon in the order of project priority, with medical personnel and hospital needs first, along with logistical experts in food shipping and distribution. Reconstruction workers, teachers, and other service providers would follow. It seemed that the Priors would fit into the latter category.

The Priors carefully filled in the applications, reporting on their work experience and language abilities. They listed their next of kin. A long section inquired about their state of health and physical characteristics, and Penny had to make precise measurements of them both to size their new uniforms. Each of them visited their family doctor to obtain a letter endorsing their general fitness for service. They also made appointments with the dentist and optometrist, and Gordon ordered two pairs of eyeglasses with an updated prescription.

They also had to be immunized against typhoid and paratyphoid and vaccinated for smallpox. Other inoculations, such as cholera, would be administered later. The smallpox vaccination, unfortunately, made Penny miserably sick for a week.

When she was well enough to be active again, they went to a photography studio for small portraits to attach to their applications and to send in with their official requests for new passports.

Reverend Prior had to obtain a letter from the Stated Clerk of his Presbytery indicating that he was a clergyman in good standing in the United Presbyterian Church of North America, or U.P.N.A. Penelope needed a letter from the Principal of Oberlin High School attesting to her graduation and good character.

Gordon Prior also had a series of negotiations with the Session of the Collegiate Presbyterian Church; he was granted a leave of absence for missionary service abroad. His salary would be suspended to enable the church to hire an interim pastor, but he would receive a stipend from the Near East Relief, which would be payable to his wife, while he would receive a small expense allowance. He also made a visit to his lawyer to set all of his affairs in order, draw up a will and update property documents, and arrange for life insurance.

The weeks slipped by as they moved through all of these steps. Penny's initial burst of enthusiasm gave way to some doubts and worries; she was afraid that she did not have enough to offer. Accustomed to self-effacement, she found it hard to present herself as a worthy member of the relief effort.

But then one day in April 1919, a thickly-stuffed envelope arrived for her from New York.

Almost unwillingly, she opened the envelope and unfolded the letter. "Dear Miss Prior," it began. "This letter notifies you that you have been duly appointed a member of the expedition in aid of displaced persons under the direction of the American Committee for Relief in the Near East, with instructions to render on behalf of the Committee such service as may be within your power in the amelioration of suffering in Western Asia. Specifically, you are expected to undertake the duties of Orphanage Assistant in Erevan, in Alexandropol, or other locations in the Republic of Armenia as may be determined by the Committee."

Penny was so excited that she had to read this message over and over to perceive even the basic sense of it. There it was, on proper letterhead stationery, with the signatures of no less than three officials of the organization, and an impressive red seal attached to the lower left corner.

She looked through the rest of the contents of the envelope. There was a long list of items to be packed, and precise dimensions for each article of luggage allowed—four suitcases or two suitcases and a trunk. The cases were to be numbered according to the degree of immediate need: suitcase number one was for supplies needed on the journey, number two for items required at destination, and thereafter for more long-term equipment such as out-of-season clothing and extra shoes. Camping cots, bedding, cooking utensils, and other standard gear were to be provided by the N.E.R.

There was a form that she needed to sign in the presence of a notary and return to the New York office accepting her appointment.

Thank you, Lord, she breathed silently. *Whatever happens, thank you for this.*

And included with this information, there was a Statement of Ideals, a sort of manifesto addressed to prospective members of the team. Penelope read, "Near East Relief is a humanitarian organization. Through the work of our dedicated officers, it is saving tens of thousands of lives. We are not content, however, with merely prolonging the physical existence of a certain number of human beings; we want not only to save life but to make life, bigger life, better life, for a better day of peace and international good will that is to come."

She continued to read, hearing a voice speaking directly to her own soul. "No one will be happy or efficient in the employ of Near East Relief who has not faced squarely the fundamental question of human life—that it is to be for others, not for self. It will appeal only to those workers who have come to the conclusion that they are in the world for what they can give and not what they can get. Near East Relief offers rich rewards beyond all material compensation, in the opportunity to save the lives of little children who would otherwise perish. It will not satisfy anyone whose major consideration is salary. It will appeal strongly to anyone whose major purpose is service."

Then there was a somewhat more ominous passage: "Near East Relief does not undertake to dictate a code of personal conduct, but it is expected that the deportment of all workers will be such as to maintain, and if possible, increase the high regard the people of the Near East have for American citizens. There are forms of behavior that under ordinary circumstances may be proper and right, but which in the Near East are not expedient. Subtle temptations, differences in ethical standards, may tend to lower ideals; home restraints are removed, no one is watching, and it is easy to compromise with high resolve. Anyone who is unable to resist such temptations should not seek appointment with the Near East Relief in any capacity either at home or abroad."

Penny was stunned by the idea that such a warning could be necessary. But in essence she was a very innocent child.

The document concluded, "To such as are willing to pay the price, we offer the chance to be true to the task of rescuing the children who will be the future of the new Near East, shaping history and ushering in a new era of security and peace."

Ten days later, Reverend Prior received his commission, and their fate was fixed.

The two of them went to the bank to sign their acceptance letters before a notary, sealed them up and mailed them. In what was for him a very unusual act of celebration, Mr. Prior took Penny to the Rexall drugstore soda fountain for a phosphate with strawberry syrup.

A date for their departure had not been set, so they needed to wait a bit longer for that information. In the meantime, they collected the items called for on their packing lists. Dr. Barton had a conversation with Gordon Prior by phone and asked him to prepare for a two-year term of service. That made their packing a rather more serious task. It was good that they had some time before sailing, since some of the articles had to be ordered in Columbus at the Marshall Field's department store.

Into Penny's trunk she placed, almost on impulse, copies of her favorite childhood books: *Anne of Green Gables*, *The Princess and the Goblin*, *The Secret Garden*, *The Blue Fairy Book*, *The Child's Dickens*, and a few others. She was not sure what use might be made of them, but somehow it seemed wrong to go without them.

On the first of June, two large cartons arrived at the house from New York. Penny opened the one addressed to her.

Inside the box she found:

> Four uniforms, two for summer and two for winter wear
> One heavy flannel union suit
> Four petticoats, one for each uniform
> Eight pairs of sturdy stockings
> One pair of boots
> One large leather handbag
> One odd-looking felt hat

She took the box up to her bedroom to examine the articles more closely.

The two summer uniforms were cut in a middy or marine style, one in khaki and one in a watery blue-green cotton. Each one came with a flimsy necktie that Penny saw at a glance could have been better designed.

She also cast a skeptical eye on the boots. They were heavy, thick-soled things with leather laces, like men's boots. In fact, they apparently were men's boots, military surplus. They were not at all like the sleek, heeled, fitted boots favored by women, with ribbons or dainty buttons. She would probably have to wear two pairs of socks at once to keep these on her feet.

The winter uniforms were better: substantial woven wool jackets in a sort of walnut brown, with wide lapels and big buttoned patch pockets, and a set-in waistband. The mid-calf skirt was widely flared and had awkward buttons all down the front. These too were military surplus, from the Women's Motor Corps of ambulance drivers now demobilized from the European war. But instead of their soft folded garrison caps, there was a wide-brimmed flat-topped hat like a park ranger's that seemed surprisingly impractical.

There were two tailored cotton shirts and two light-brown neckties to wear with the winter uniforms. The handbag was big, square, and plain, like a messenger bag.

But the detail she did like very much was the patch sewn on to the left sleeves: a big white five-pointed star inside a circle, with the letters N.E.R.

stitched onto it. The hat also had a star patch right in the center of the crown. Seeing that patch gave her a little thrill of pride.

She put on all of the components of one of the winter uniforms to see how they fit.

A narrow mirror hung upon the door of Penelope's wardrobe. She stood before it and regarded herself critically. The wispy hair, not quite blond; the hazel eyes, not quite green; the pale skin, soft like a child's. She felt herself to be as colorless as a ghost. And that stalky body . . . some girls had what was often described as a generous bosom, but hers was just the opposite. She detested her own appearance as only an unforgiving teenager can do. But any other person saw a slender, delicately pretty girl who seemed younger than her years.

While she was standing before her mirror thinking about this, the bedroom door opened and in came her sister Matilda. She stopped short in surprise, then smiled.

"Pardon me, officer," she said, "I was looking for my sister Penelope."

They laughed. Penny turned around so her sister could look at the uniform. "Well, Tildy? What do you think?"

"It's not the most flattering outfit I've ever seen. But you know what? I like it anyway."

"That's very much the way I feel, too. It makes it seem like I'm really a part of this effort, now . . . like what I'm trying to do really is important."

"What's that expression, 'Clothes make the man'? Or woman? Perhaps for women it matters even more."

"Well, if there is that much riding on it, I'm going to have to alter those dreadful summer uniforms. Aren't they ugly? I'm guessing that the woolen ones are military issue, and that they've had a few years to make them look decent. But maybe these light-weight ones were thrown together quickly because someone realized that summers are *hot* in the Near East."

"I wonder how much of the time you will wear your uniform. Are there working hours? May you dress as you like while off duty?"

"They say one should pack one's own normal clothing as well. And of course, if there is something else I need, I can always sew it myself."

"Can we send you packages, Pen? What if I put some embroidery floss in a letter and mail it to you?"

"Who knows, Tildy? Perhaps it's like mailing things to soldiers at the front."

Matilda suddenly went silent. When Penny looked at her more closely, she saw that her sister was weeping.

"Tildy, Tildy, please don't," said Penny, embracing her.

"It's like you *are* a soldier going to the front," Matilda whispered. "We don't know how dangerous it may be out there. Missionaries and aid workers have died in the relief already, from disease and accidents and who knows what. Our Auntie Nan barely survived the war. What if I don't ever see you again?"

"That's not the right way to think, surely. I believe the Lord is sending me there to do something useful, not just to get hit by a train."

"Those others probably believed so, too."

"All right, enough of that. How am I going to say goodbye to you, and to James, and to little Max and Wally, if we're having all of these morbid thoughts?"

Matilda said no more about it, but that did not mean she stopped feeling this way.

That very same day, a telegram was delivered to Gordon Prior at the Collegiate Church. He brought it home directly and read it to them all. REPORT NY OFFICE ACRNE 151 FIFTH AVENUE 26 JUNE 1919 SAIL 30 JUNE USS HAMILTON TO BREST.

Mixed emotions swirled around the supper table that night, and later, while giving Max and Wally their bath and reading them stories. Before Penny came to bed, Matilda quietly cried herself to sleep.

CHAPTER 2

PARTING with the family at the railway station was likewise a mixed experience. The younger children clung to Penny like a life-raft . . . even James, a boy of fourteen who might have been beyond all that.

Wellandette had already discovered that sacrificing her husband and eldest child to save lives in Asia greatly enhanced her own social standing with the Mrs. Blairs and Mrs. Howells of Oberlin. This public role required a suitable dramatic performance on the train platform. Had Penny been less awash in her own feelings, she might have noticed Gordon Prior's lighter step upon bidding farewell to his wife for a period of two years.

The train trip to New York City was uneventful, apart from Reverend Prior's habit of preaching at all times and in all places, especially when anyone mentioned the victory of the Allies in the war. He felt it was his duty to explain why and how God had enabled this great triumph of righteousness over Prussian militarism and barbarism.

"The German, Austrian and Turkish hordes were motivated only by greed and the desire for conquest," he would say. "The lust for power is the only thing that moves them, while selfless purpose inspires us. The enemy had nothing that we desire, neither territory nor wealth, and those whom we were defending likewise have nothing that we want. We act only to rescue and redeem. Beyond doubt, our pure purpose has received Divine approval. God could not express Himself in antagonism to this end. Therefore, His will has been enacted and evil defeated, and it must always ultimately be so."

At about this point, his listeners would decide to finish their meal and get out of the dining car, and Penny took refuge in reading *Wuthering Heights*.

They arrived in New York as planned on the twenty-sixth of June, making their way to the Near East Relief offices, receiving there a cordial welcome. They surrendered the bags and trunks that needed to be stowed below during the voyage. A friendly young woman took them to their temporary lodging in the guest house and encouraged them to enjoy the life and sights of New York, which for a couple of days they did.

On that Sunday, they attended the Brick Presbyterian Church at Fifth Avenue and 37th Street. The pastor made the mistake of asking Reverend Prior to say a few words.

And then, on Monday, 30 June 1919, they donned their summer uniforms and embarked upon the *USS Hamilton*. And the adventure well and truly began.

Penny thrilled to the touch of the deck of the oceangoing vessel under her feet.

With some effort they located their billets. The ship was stuffed to the gills with cargo, allowing the smallest space possible for the accommodation of the 170 human beings aboard. She found her little room and opened the door.

A woman in uniform was sitting on the lower bunk, going through her handbag. "Oh, hello!" she said brightly, looking up at her.

"Good morning," Penny responded. "I think I'm supposed to be in this room."

"Yes, welcome. You're Penelope Prior, it says on this list. I'm Jane Eberlee. I don't need to be in this lower bunk, if you would prefer it."

"No, not at all, please don't move," Penny said, as Jane got up. "I can sleep anywhere, I don't mind."

"Well, I can too, at this point in my life. I learned to sleep sitting up in the hospital during my residency. They could stack me in the cargo hold and I'd be all right."

Penny asked the obvious question. "You're a doctor?"

"Yes, I am now. I've just finished my residency in family practice and pediatrics. I would have signed up sooner for this mission if I could have. But I had to complete my training first."

"Oh," said Penny. She realized that the polite thing to do would be to offer some information about herself, but she couldn't think of anything interesting to say. "I'm . . . an Orphanage Assistant."

"That's wonderful, I'm so happy to hear it. I believe they've assigned all of us staff for the Caucasus together. I must say though, this uniform certainly looks better on you than it does on me. I feel like I'm standing here in a flour sack."

"They're not very well tailored, are they? I admit, I altered mine quite a bit."

"Did you? Clever with a needle, eh? How lucky I am to be in this room. Perhaps you'll consider working some magic on mine as well," Jane Eberlee smiled.

"I don't have a sewing machine available . . . but I can probably improve things a little with just my hand-sewing kit," Penny said.

"Oh, I'd be much obliged. I never learned anything about clothing. But if you need a wound sutured, I'm at your service."

"I certainly hope I won't."

"One never knows! I think we're to assemble soon in the dining area."

They did assemble, gradually, for a general orientation. Leaders of the Near East Relief went over much of the same information that had been sent to them in writing. They laid out the schedule for the weeks of the voyage. Their days would be largely devoted to detailed briefings from area coordinators on conditions and expectations in their various geographic areas: the city of Constantinople, the Black Sea coast, south central Anatolia and Buraan, the eastern frontier, and the lower Caucasus. Staff heading to Syria were sent on separate ships to Beirut.

Intensive language training would occupy much of this time. Penny learned that she had been assigned to serve as an Armenian language instructor, leading one of the conversational groups that would drill the Caucasus contingent in words and phrases to be memorized. This adult role pleased her immensely.

The whole group did a lot of milling about, visiting and getting to know each other, and Penny eventually discovered that only fourteen of them had been appointed to serve in Armenia. She asked her roommate Jane Eberlee if she knew why.

Doctor Eberlee hesitated a moment before answering. "Well . . . here's what I know. I'm actually a member of the American Women's Hospitals organization, seconded to the Near East Relief. When they were looking for physicians to join up, they made it clear that they would not choose people for Armenia—one had to volunteer. Because it is considered especially hazardous duty."

Penny learned more about this at the first meeting of the Caucasus group, led by Ernest Yarrow, the N.E.R. Director for the region.

"Ladies and gentlemen, thank you for making yourselves available to the relief effort in the Republic of Armenia. To have such capable people come out and join us in our situation . . . it's more meaningful than I can say. Like many of you, I am a former missionary, at the Protestant College in Van. We were driven out in the summer of 1917, and I've been helping to organize the relief effort since then. In February, some of us went out in the *Pensacola* to Beirut to make a detailed assessment of need. I came back for consultations in New York three months ago, and now I'm returning to the field. The Committee has been trying to develop a plan for dealing with the . . . the catastrophe that is Armenia."

The atmosphere in the room was deeply serious. "The Armenians forced out of eastern Anatolia roughly doubled the population of the Caucasus region. But this was not a settled, productive population . . . it was over 400,000 destitute and traumatized refugees. They poured into a region that had already been trampled by war, scorched by retreating armies. The land could not sustain the permanent residents, let alone the refugees. And then, the winter of 1918–19 was one of the most severe on record. Long, harsh, arid, freezing cold . . . no food or shelter, no clothing, every street filled with desperate and dying people. Hundreds perished each day. Entire villages emptied. I have not the words to tell you how devastating it was."

He breathed slowly. "You know, of course, that the mission of our organization is not so much general relief, but specifically the care of separated and orphaned children. I must commend the American Relief Administration for their help in transporting large quantities of relief goods to Armenia, especially grain. There was no grain harvest at all last year and there will be very little this summer. We helped as much as we could with the distribution work.

"Our chief effort has been to find locations for the countless children living on the streets and in dreadful temporary shelters in Erevan, Alexandropol, Kars, Igdir, Echmiadzin. I want you all to understand that you are not going out to take your place in functioning institutions. In most cases, nothing like a proper orphanage yet exists. We need to reconstruct buildings, establish feeding and medical centers, open schools. We have made a little progress since the first N.E.R. supplies and appointed personnel arrived in March . . . but there is so much further to go."

He looked at each of them. "You must be prepared to do whatever is necessary to reclaim the ruined buildings we have taken on . . . to rescue children in the most extreme state of malnutrition and disease . . . to realize that everything you do, to the utmost of your power, will be only a scratch upon the surface of the urgent need.

"Your group is small on this voyage because we cannot sustain our staff adequately in the field as yet. You have been chosen because you have skills that are very much needed. I regret that . . . this means the burdens on you will be even greater, with a shortage of staff and poor support for your own daily needs. Please know that we are attempting to increase personnel numbers and minimal conditions for sustaining them, as quickly as we can."

Penny was beginning to realize that her mental image of stepping into a new role in an established and organized setting would need to be revised. She left the meeting with a great deal to think about.

When the first Armenian language class convened, she found that it was to be led by a Protestant teacher from Central Turkey College in Aintab, who had been deported in 1915 and escaped through Syria, eventually to the United States. Sahag Asdourian was eager to get to the newly-formed Republic of Armenia and contribute to the rebuilding of its society. He asked Penny to take notes during class and then go over the lesson repeatedly with half of the group while he drilled the other half himself.

They started with the Armenian alphabet, a collection of squiggles that struck fear into the hearts of the less linguistically-inclined among them. Then Mr. Asdourian began teaching them simple words and phrases . . . hello, *barev dzez* . . . how are you, *inchpes es* . . . I'm fine, *lav em* . . . please, *khindrum em* . . . and then they all ran aground on thank you, *shnorhagalutyun*. In their sections, they practiced these and variants on them, until the students were *barev*-ing each other with some degree of confidence.

When the class was dismissed, the teacher thanked Penny for her help, and they went over the next lesson together. She said then in Armenian, "Mr. Asdourian, I want to tell you . . . that I am so sorry for everything you have been through, you and your family and friends and community. I am so very sorry."

His eyes filled with tears and he turned away. "God bless you," he said.

They became an effective teaching team. There were also briefings about politics, geography, history, and culture. Dr. Eberlee and the three nurses in the Caucasus unit asked for special training in medical terminology, so they prepared another set of lessons for them.

Reverend Prior felt somewhat overlooked in this training period, since he considered himself an authority on the Armenian nation. But his language skills tended toward the literary and formal, and his colloquial Armenian was actually rather weak. Having learned the language as an adult, he spoke stiffly and with a definite accent. Penny, on the other hand, spoke the language from her cradle, learning it through her Armenian nurses and nannies in Tabriz. She had easy fluency and the natural sound of a native speaker, though in the vernacular dialect common in northern Persia. Gordon found it a little galling to be outdone by his own daughter.

The group also took their meals together. One evening, conversation turned to the moral lessons of the Great War, and suddenly Gordon Prior was in his element.

"The Church has been most loyal, in the sending forth of her sons as a sacrifice upon the altar of the nation. Patriotism may be an old-fashioned sentiment, but there are no greater words in our language than God and Home and Country," Gordon said.

"The war was a crusade to save Christian civilization," someone else offered. "From the atrocities of wicked men. Clearly, the Allies were brandished as a sword by God to defend order, law, and virtue from the gross criminality of the Germans and the Turks."

"Why yes, and we must not lose sight of the fact that it was really in the interest of the German people that the German armies should be defeated," another person, a gentleman Penny knew as Mr. Whitney, chimed in. "They needed to be released from the domination of their false ideals. And the madness of their misguided leaders. There was no other way, surely."

"Indeed," Gordon Prior responded. "Why has the Almighty endowed *us* with the strength to oppose their evil plans? As a young and powerful nation of Christian principles, the United States of America has been providentially created for the purpose of fighting the great battle for civilization. I find no trace of virtue in any aim of the Germans or the Turks. They mean no benefit to anyone but themselves. Any force they can conceive of they will apply against those they wish to overwhelm and destroy," stated Prior, warming to his subject. "Peace with such powers cannot be secured by mere submission. To lie down before aggression is to accept the doctrine that might makes right."

"Whilst wielding our own might in order to do it," said a soft voice with a British accent. "And committing our own atrocities in the process." Penny leaned forward to look at a quiet young man with eyeglasses whom she had not noticed before.

"Nonsense, lad. The Allies displayed only the gallantry of the hero in the face of a morally degraded foe."

"That was not the way I experienced it," said the quiet voice again.

"But of course, one must consider the larger view," Prior went on. "We had to win the war to free the world. Our stewardship rests not in the perfection of persons, but in the superiority of our ideals. Service with disinterested motives is naturally pure. Regrettably, meeting violence with violence will never be a pretty sight, yet upon the consecrated fields of Belgium and of France, the baptism of fire was a cleansing force. In the glory of the trenches, the very faces of the victorious soldiers were ennobled by the beauty of the ideals for which they fought."

The young man coughed awkwardly. "I must admit, I never saw a beautiful soldier in the trenches. Not from any nation."

"We are speaking of spiritual beauty—of noble purpose."

"I was in the trenches at the Somme, at Mametz Wood, at Ypres and at Passchendaele. In the midst of the constant bombardment, the artillery shells, the machine-gun fire, noble purpose was perhaps the last thing on our minds."

"The warrior is himself a bit too close to the action to grasp the concept of the whole," Gordon replied, undeterred. "It is for us to interpret to them the ultimate meaning of their own experience."

The young man's face went blank, and after a moment he got up to clear his dishes. "If you will excuse me," he murmured. Penny watched him leave the room, waited for the attention of others to be diverted, then got up to follow him.

She found him not far away on the deck, leaning on the rail, looking out at the darkening sea. Tentatively, she went over and joined him.

"I thought I was the only one who does this," she began.

The young man smiled apologetically, then shifted their positions so she was standing at his right instead of his left.

"Sorry," he said. "What was that again?"

"I said, I thought I was the only one who does this."

"Does what, now?" he asked warily.

"This," she replied. "Going off alone to fume at the things my parents say. I don't know how you could be so polite to him. It's infuriating, the way he always thinks he knows your own business better than you do yourself."

"I admit I couldn't have stayed in the room for very much longer," he said.

Her voice was suddenly angry. "My father is a pompous, pedantic old—blowhard!"

"Wait wait *wait* a moment, there."

"Oh, I've just had too much of it. You can't imagine."

"I think we can perhaps reshape this a little for you. Pompous? Well, he is a member of a profession which is vested with considerable authority . . . whether they deserve it or not. Perhaps people expect that, or demand it of him. Pedantic? He's well educated and knowledgeable. Only—*not* about trench warfare," he said with a wry smile.

"You must have suffered a great deal during . . . all of that."

"Well, I did manage to extend things a bit, enlisting in 1914. I suppose smarter people waited to be called up. I saw very steady action until Passchendaele. After that I was demobbed with disability. That was in the autumn of 1917. I've been in New York since then."

Penny felt she should not ask, then did anyway. "Disability?"

"Yes . . . first I was shot through the calf, right here, but as soon as it healed over I was sent out again. Then I came down with trench fever. Sick as a bloody dog—pardon my language. But once I could move around, back to the fray I went. What did it for me was this," he said, pointing to his left ear. "Shell exploded too close. Concussed, out like a light. They actually left me for dead. I was picked up by the graves detail, and luckily they found I had a pulse. But the eardrum is gone. Deaf as a post on that side. Turns out there is an army reg prohibiting the deaf from serving in the infantry . . . probably the officers are afraid we wouldn't hear them yelling, 'Over the top!'"

"Forgive me . . . perhaps it's hard for you to talk about."

"Oh, I got over that long ago. Americans are so direct, you see. If they want to know something, they simply come right out and ask."

She looked away, embarrassed.

"It's all right. Talking to you is like talking to my little sister."

This annoyed Penny a bit, as she was sensitive about being much younger than most of the workers appointed to the relief service. She tried to suppress the feeling. "Are you close to your younger sister?"

"I haven't got a younger sister. But if I had, I imagine she'd be something like you."

"Well, since I'm asking direct questions, what were you doing in New York?"

"I'm an engraver and illustrator. Some painting as well, and book design. Camberwell School of Arts and Crafts. I went back there after my discharge, but there was very little going on in the publishing field in England during the war, so I made my way to Madison Avenue with the other artists who sell themselves to the advertising industry. I'm not above making my living through commercial art, you understand, but it soon seemed clear that drawing ads for cigarettes and baby shoes was not going to work for me for very long. So that's when I found a place in printing and learned to use a Gestetner press."

"To use a what?"

"A Gestetner. It's a new technology for making quick duplicates of documents. You can use a typewriter to cut a stencil, then run off copies of it—very much in demand for office work. I've brought one along, with Remington and Underhill typewriters. That's how I ended up here, in fact."

"I don't follow you."

"Well, the Near East Relief sent out word among the print shops that they needed people to come out and create instructional materials for teaching school in the orphanages. Where textbooks are few and far between. Can't teach kids to read if they have nothing to read, now can you?"

Penny began to put two and two together. "Oh, dear."

"So, you have grasped the situation. I'm supposed to be the publishing partner of the Reverend Gordon Prior, churning out schoolbooks for the children of Armenia. Working hand in glove, so to speak. You see now why it's quite important for both of us to learn to get along with your father." They both smiled.

"I'm sorry," said Penny, apologizing again, "but I don't recognize you. You are not in my half of the Armenian language class."

"No, lucky for you. I'm not an apt pupil of languages. My name's Arnaud."

"That's . . . Mr. Arno?" she asked, guessing from the pronunciation. She couldn't tell if it was a given name or a surname. Only later, when she looked at the staff roster, did she learn how it was spelled. On the roster his first name appeared as D.

"Just Arnaud. Assume that I have no given name. Even my closest friends call me simply Arnaud."

And they were fast friends from that day onward. Arnaud did treat her like a younger sister, and Penny had the chance to experience the older sibling she had never had. Jane Eberlee immediately joined their friendship as well. The rest of the voyage passed very pleasantly, even though Gordon Prior never stopped pontificating in the dining room.

A few days before they stopped at Brest to take on fuel and fresh provisions and to drop off transatlantic mail, on the seventeenth of July, Jane and Arnaud surprised Penny with a birthday party.

"Hail the birthday girl, now a sweet seventeen!" Arnaud joked. "Seventeen on the seventeenth."

"Does everyone have to keep reminding me about my age? I don't comment about how old all of you people are."

"It's nothing to be embarrassed about," said Ernest Yarrow, the Caucasus Director. "The Niles survey team we sent out to eastern Anatolia . . . their photographer, name of Sutherland, was also seventeen years old. He did a fine job. He actually wrote the team report, since Captain Niles wasn't one for keeping notes and such."

Mr. Asdourian taught them all to say, "*Tsinunded Shnorhavor!*" Happy Birthday! And they toasted her with bottled lemon juice mixed with sugar and soda water. The galley managed to produce a decent chocolate cake. And Mr. Whitney, the senior inventory manager, had brought along his violin, so there was some nice music, and even a little dancing.

But as they left Brest and moved down the Atlantic coast of France, Spain, and Portugal, the atmosphere aboard became increasingly tense. There were serious briefings from Mr. Yarrow about the details of the mission they were undertaking. He issued to each of them a Sam Browne belt—a wide leather buckled belt around the waist with a narrower band across the right shoulder—and a service revolver, with a closed leather holster.

"You won't be wearing these all the time. But when you need to leave the compounds and travel in contested areas, each of you must be armed. If you've never used a weapon before, there will be training sessions, led by one of our veterans, Mr. Arnaud."

"A Sam Browne belt . . . at last, this is my chance to dress like an officer," Arnaud muttered to Penny.

As they reached Gibraltar and passed into the Mediterranean, their progress slowed, and at night nearly stopped, due to the risk of floating mines. And when they reached the Aegean Sea, they were joined by six small craft doing an intensive mine watch, all the way up through the Dardanelles, past Gallipoli, and into the Sea of Marmara.

They passed the city of Constantinople on an overcast day with a drizzle of rain, when the view of it from the ship was not the best. But even then they could catch a glimpse of its unique beauty. "There will be no stopping there on this trip, I'm afraid," Mr. Yarrow had told them. "No time for sightseeing. The cargo on this vessel is so urgently needed that any delay means prolonged suffering and lives lost. We are now in a race to get these supplies to those who need them." The weeks at sea in a timeless bubble were over. Now the sense of working under pressure would affect everything they could do.

The *Hamilton* proceeded toward the east through the narrow but very deep Gulf of Ismid to the heavy-goods port of Derindje, where it docked at last.

The German army had built two enormous stone warehouses at Derindje, one of them six stories and the other four stories tall. The Kaiser had used this port to supply their ally Turkey with every kind of military equipment during the war, from Mauser bolt-action rifles to locomotives.

On one side of these huge warehouses was the harbor, with docks that could accommodate ocean-going vessels. On the other side was a major rail complex, with six tracks where freight trains could be loaded, and switching links to the trunk lines of the Anatolian Railway.

The Near East Relief had taken possession of the entire dock area and a constant stream of supplies and equipment was already underway. The *Hamilton* would contribute its cargo to this stream, as well as its human cargo of relief workers, who were accommodated in primitive conditions on the top floors of the warehouses until they could be shuffled off to their various destinations in Turkey's interior.

The three inventory managers in their number quickly organized twenty-four-hour work parties, supervising the physical unloading of goods from the hold of the *Hamilton* into the warehouses. More than two hundred Turkish laborers were employed to do the carrying, in exchange for bread and several liras per day; many more men pressed against the locked gates of the warehouse compound, hoping for a chance to do this work. A tall wire fence topped with barbed wire surrounded the area.

Some of the laborers were assigned to move the passengers and their luggage into the warehouses, hoisting heavy trunks on their backs and climbing six flights of stairs to the women's quarters and four flights up to the men's. Penny and Jane discovered rows of Army cots for fifty women in a bare attic space, hot and stuffy, with no running water or toilets; washstands with pitchers and basins, and kerosene cans half-full of water were the only sanitary means available. Fresh water was delivered and slops carried away once a day.

The women already staying in this dormitory showed them where to establish themselves, making many jokes about the Ritz-Carlton Hotel. The so-called restaurant was a battered wooden shack where food was served cafeteria-style whenever anyone could take a break long enough to eat.

In the heavy, hand-to-hand work of unloading, it was impossible to keep the various goods organized. Men trudged back and forth with construction tools and farm implements, crates of medical supplies, tins of kerosene, bales of secondhand clothing, blankets, generators, water pumps and other machinery, glassware, cutlery and crockery, sheets and towels, laundry equipment, pharmaceuticals, cleaning and sterilizing gear. Then ton after ton of corn grits, beans, wheat flour, sugar, lard, and countless cans of meat and condensed milk. All of these were stacked in the warehouses, back to front, in a sort of controlled chaos.

It was the task of the relief workers to unpack all of these goods and repack them into the correct assortments for their various destinations.

They prepared loads of goods for trains to Konya, Marash and Sivas, each train provided with boxcars for the N.E.R. staff to travel in, sleeping on Army cots, sitting on crates and trunks. A boxcar with camp stoves was set up for cooking and sharing meals. Each train traveled with an armed detachment to guard it day and night. They had a boxcar to bunk in, too.

The boxcars were small and balanced very high on big metal wheels, with the floor of the car at waist level; a stair or rung was often built into the side below the sliding door to allow someone to step up and into the car. Even so, for the smaller members of the team it took an effort just to climb in and out.

The Caucasus crew ended up doing much more than their share of this endless unpacking, sorting, repacking, and loading of goods, because they were stranded in Derindje waiting for a vessel to take them to Batoum. Weeks after their arrival in Turkey, they were still doing warehouse duty in eight-hour shifts around the clock.

The train yard was outside the warehouse area and not surrounded by fences, because the trains had to be able to move in and out. That meant there was no way to fend off the steady incursion of hungry people who furtively occupied the rail yard. They begged for bread, they waited for any kind of food to fall from the boxcars, for a sack of flour to split and dump part of its contents onto the ground, where it was quickly scooped up and carried away.

Patrols of Turkish police were supposed to keep those people away from the rails for their own safety. But as soon as they shooed some away, more of them took their place.

Mr. Whitney and the other two inventory managers were becoming exhausted. Their constant vigilance and attention to every detail was taking a toll. They rotated the difficult overnight shifts, but never did get as much rest as they really needed.

One damp night Mr. Whitney was on duty when they were making final checks on a train due to depart for the Marsovan area first thing in the morning. He needed to be sure that the boxcars were properly sealed before the train moved out of the loading area and into the boarding zone.

He was working from one car to the next, attending to his ever-present clipboard with its pages and pages of lading lists, when he became aware of something moving under the car. The light was very poor on that end of the yard; the globe lantern he carried cast just enough light for him to see that there was a huddle of children hiding under its wheels.

"What are you doing down there?" he exclaimed. "Get out of there right now! This train is about to move!" In his alarm, he was yelling at them in English, as not a single word of Turkish or Armenian could be summoned to his mind. His yelling only frightened them and they shrank back further under the car.

"Come on now, come out this way, quick, quick!" he urged, dropping the clipboard and lantern and reaching out his hands to them.

At that moment, the train gave a sudden lurch forward and knocked him to the ground, then rolled over his body as he lay upon the tracks.

As dawn was breaking, someone spotted what they took to be a lost duffle bag or a bundle of old clothes that had fallen from a boxcar. They discovered what was left of Whitney. The Turkish police and the U.S. Embassy stepped in. They had a procedure for dealing with the remains of altruistic Americans who had given their lives in an effort to save the world.

CHAPTER 3

SHORTLY after they lost Whitney, a ship was found to transport them and their goods to Batoum. Functional vessels were scarce, and Turkish owners had little interest in transporting supplies to their enemies in Armenia. Contracts were arranged and then fell through. Ernest Yarrow simmered with frustration at the delay, while essential goods remained in the warehouses at Derindje.

The two remaining inventory managers, Shears and Costen, went to twelve-hour shifts to load the ship as quickly as possible. Arnaud and Prior shadowed them and filled in when they needed a break.

The ship was a filthy old coal transport out of Bulgaria, but it would have to do. Crew quarters were so humble that they nearly did make the warehouse dormitories seem like the Ritz-Carlton in comparison. But it had a large, stable, reinforced hold for their tons of food and equipment.

Ernest Yarrow spoke to the gathered Caucasus team on the deck, since there was no other space big enough for them all. "I've got your specific location assignments now. We have thirty-two N.E.R. staff at this point in Armenia, mostly in the towns along the rail corridor. Relief activities there are ongoing. So your group will be sent to the newly-acquired military barracks beyond Alexandropol, where the government has given us access to a huge complex that we need to turn into safe accommodation for homeless children."

"Did you say military barracks?"

"Yes . . . it's an extraordinary site, built by the Tsar almost a century ago for his armies holding the frontier against the Ottomans. Three very extensive barracks compounds. Scores of buildings, mostly solid structures of dressed stone. But they are not in a ready condition for the most part. We will need to use all of the construction materials we are bringing with us to whip them into shape as soon as possible. That will be the job of our three engineers, Franklin, Brownlea and Merle."

"What will we have for labor, or for skilled craftsmen?" asked Brownlea.

"There is a sizable contingent of workers, adult men paid with rations of corn grits. Among them are some carpenters, mechanics, plumbers and others with decent skills. Eight N.E.R. staff are already on site, including one handyman mechanic. He's got several buildings at Kazachi Post ready for occupancy . . . that is, after a fashion," Yarrow said, with a diffident gesture, almost a shrug.

"That is to say, there are roofs, doors and windows, and running water. The Kazachi Post site has an excellent water supply. You must understand, these barracks were well built, but they've been empty for a while, and occupied by soldiers passing through, who left an ungodly mess behind. Woodwork torn out and burned, rubbish everywhere, general disorder. Every building needs restoration. But we can't wait till they are shipshape before using them for shelter. Last I heard, there were three thousand orphaned children there already."

"Three *thousand?*" exclaimed one of the nurses, Miss Webster.

"Oh, that's only the beginning. There are thousands upon thousands more, desperately in need. Not just homeless—also starved and sick. Dr. Eberlee, you will join Dr. Artine Der Ghazarian and Dr. Peter Ruhl, the eye surgeon, as chief medical staff. Miss Webster, you will also be at Kazachi Post, with the two nurses who are there now. Miss Finn and Miss Hickson, you will be at the other two barracks centers, Seversky Post and Polygon, to begin setting them up for medical services."

"Where is the nearest hospital?" asked Jane Eberlee.

Yarrow looked at her a moment. "There is an intake center where children are cared for when they first arrive. But the whole population is in need of treatment . . . the whole camp is a hospital, in that sense."

They were stealing glances at one another.

"Kazachi Post is at the end of a spur track of the rail line, with secure stone warehouses nearby, so that has become the central stockpile for supplies. Shears and Costen will oversee unloading. I'm not sure how well staffed they are at the Post for inventory management right now, so if needed, I hope you gentlemen will assist," he said, speaking to Arnaud and Prior.

The docks at Batoum were much smaller than those at Derindje, and the warehouses were all privately owned, so they planned to unload their cargo directly into freight cars. But of course, the train they needed was not yet ready, and they had to wait several more days. Then it was their turn to experience the joys of boxcar travel.

The train moved slowly, since the track in many places was in a dubious condition. There was always a risk of derailing caused by damage or obstacles on the rail line. But during the day they could open the sliding doors of their boxcar dormitory and their dining car, where their Armenian cook kept camp stoves going with tea, cocoa and an indistinguishable stew. They could sit on crates and watch the very rugged mountainous landscape of Georgia go by.

When it got dark they had to stop, enclosed inside their cars, the sliding doors barricaded with iron bars, and their armed escort patrolling all night. Due to congestion on the track ahead at Tiflis, they had to stop one night at the edge of a destitute and nearly ruined town. When they had gone to bed, Penny began to hear a rustling noise, and then a soft patting or tapping on the outside of their car. Then she heard voices . . . hushed pleading voices, begging for food. They were being very quiet in order to avoid bringing the guards down on them. When they were chased away, they moved to the back side of the boxcar and started again, with a low inarticulate wailing sound.

"Jane!" Penny whispered. "Jane, are you awake? Can you hear that?"

"Yes," she whispered back. "It's terrible."

"Can't we do something? They're starving. We've got food."

"We can't open the cars at night. It's too dangerous."

"But . . . *listen*," Penny said.

"I know," Jane replied, in a choked voice.

They lay on their cots in the darkness of the boxcar, listening to the other women around them breathing in their sleep, and the hungry people outside, moaning.

Once they reached the rail corridor connecting the major cities of Armenia, the wretched condition of the people was overwhelming. Train stations were concentration points for those hoping for some kind of assistance, or perhaps travel out to a better place; but when that hope went unfulfilled, the stations also served as camps for the despairing and the dying.

The N.E.R. used the stations as feeding centers, setting up soup kitchens for the general population, well away from the tracks, cooking masses of corn grits into a bland but digestible porridge. The Caucasus train delivered an allotted portion of their supplies to each of these points and checked on the status of the N.E.R. staff coping with this task.

They continued their supply voyage out to Alexandropol, the last town of any size on the lower Caucasus route, and then a few miles beyond it to a broad, empty, treeless plain ringed with mountains. In 1837, Tsar Nicholas the First had chosen this area to establish three extensive military bases: Kazachi Post for his Cossack cavalry, Seversky Post for the infantry, and Polygon for the artillery units. They constructed impressive buildings of black volcanic rock with red roof tiles and brick trim, many long one- and two-story regimental barracks, stables, storerooms, officers' quarters and many support structures, some 140 solid stone buildings, housing thousands of Russian soldiers.

The Tsar also built a remarkable symbol of his imperial reach, there at Kazachi Post—an imposing Orthodox church. Large, ornate, with two tall towers. One tower had a classic Russian onion dome, the other a tapering conical tower traditional in churches of the Caucasus. Smaller onion domes, a bell tower, decorative architectural detail ... the church seemed an incongruous apparition from another world in that stark utilitarian setting.

After the Russo-Turkish War ending in 1878, the military complex fell slowly into disuse, and the buildings began to deteriorate. Regiments passing through used them for shelter, but with no incentive to maintain the complex, those occupants hastened its decline.

Local relief workers reclaimed some of the buildings to house the crowds of refugees who poured into Armenia during the Great War, but without proper supplies they struggled. Orphaned girls were packed into a few buildings at Kazachi Post, and boys at Polygon.

"Jane! Arnaud! Look! You can see the barracks now. Goodness, so many rows of buildings. And a beautiful church there behind them."

They were standing in the open doorway of the dining boxcar as the train slowly pulled into its final destination at the end of the spur track. "They've formed a reception committee," said Arnaud, gesturing at the group of people waiting beside the train.

"I imagine that the arrival of a supply train is a major event here," observed Jane.

Very quickly, people were helping them to climb down from their cars, picking up their baggage and camp cots and carrying it all for them. "Am I ever happy to see *you*," said a smiling young man of about thirty, extending his hand to Arnaud.

Ernest Yarrow happened to be standing next to him at the time. "Arnaud, this is Rufus Kendrick, the mechanic on site," he said.

"Ah," replied Arnaud. "In that case, I believe it is these three gentlemen whom you are happy to see," he said, indicating Franklin, Brownlea, and Merle, the construction engineers.

"I'm happy to see *all* of you, to be honest," said Kendrick eagerly. "We've been so short-handed here at the end of the world."

The new arrivals were taken to a building at one end of the parade ground that was in reasonably intact condition—the officers' quarters. The thirteen new staff members were squeezed into all available corners, after some shifting around, as those who had made friends during the voyage tried to share the same rooms. Penny and Jane ended up in a little space with Fran Webster.

Mr. Yarrow stayed for one more day, and then went on to the other stations in his district.

Their workday began at dawn, with cocoa, porridge, and a much-appreciated treat: little soft loaves of fresh bread. The wheat flour they had brought was already being put to use. Jane Eberlee and Frannie Webster were whisked off at once to the intake hospital, the engineers to high-priority projects expanding the bakery and water-heating systems, and all other able-bodied persons to another urgent task. They were to help with the cleaning and repair of a building needed for an inpatient and ambulatory clinic.

Penny longed to get directly involved in the care of the children she had come so far to help. But she understood that the staff on site knew what kind of assistance they needed most.

"I regret that we must begin here, with a truly distasteful task," said the Ward Matron, Miss Dirouhi. "But our need for more space for the sick is paramount. We have no rooms for isolation of those with communicable diseases, separate from the patients needing surgery or medical treatment. Our plan is to set up dedicated facilities at Seversky Post for trachoma patients—one of those infections that spread so rapidly among children. But for now, we must use the floors of this building to provide places for them."

The two-story stone building did have doors and window frames, though no glass panes as yet. But when they entered, they met a squad of Armenian laborers carrying out chunks of broken furniture, crushed empty tins, and heaps of other junk. The largest ward space had been cleared of rubbish, but Penny soon saw that it was far from empty: on the floors and walls moved masses of lice and fleas and roaches and bedbugs, swarming in chaotic motion in and out of cracks and corners.

"Heavenly days!" said Penny, a pastor's daughter incapable of profanity.

"Reminds me of the Somme," joked Arnaud.

"It's a good thing we brought all of that Lysol," she replied.

Someone thrust brooms and empty kerosene tins into their hands, and the battle was on.

They spent most of the day sweeping up vast numbers of insects, filling their kerosene tins and then pouring them into tubs filled with water and Lysol, where the bugs died a lingering death. As soon as they had swept, they washed all of the surfaces, using buckets and mops full of Lysol and water right up to the ceilings. The taller men climbed up on crates to mop the ceilings and were rewarded with a shower of disinfectant and not a few errant insects.

Penny quickly made friends with the many Armenian workers scrubbing alongside them. She was especially impressed with the Matron, Miss Dirouhi, who was directing their efforts. The Matron patiently kept everyone going, cheering them up at times with encouraging words.

Mr. Kendrick, who was somehow managing to be everywhere at once, brought them more equipment.

"Here you are, then," he said with a touch of pride. "This is our method for killing the little buggers inside the walls where they hide. These are Pyro fire extinguishers we salvaged from our Ford trucks. They're filled with a mixture of bichloride of mercury and soap. You need to spray every visible seam and crack, so that it soaks in well. Then, when it dries, it makes a hard crust that seals them into their nests."

"Ingenious," said Arnaud.

"Perhaps the trait we need most in this job is creative thinking," Kendrick said.

"And the stomach to scoop up roaches by the quart," added Penny.

When at last they stopped for the day, Arnaud took Penny aside. "Listen, there is no possible way that we failed to pick up some passengers today, doing all of that. When you remove your clothes, examine every stitch, and then run a lighted candle over the seams. Try not to set fire to the garment, of course. But heat the seams well, and if you hear any little snapping sounds like popcorn, do it again. Kendrick says they have only one steam delouser set up so far and it's in great demand. But this will help."

"Thanks. I'll meet you at dinner, if I can still stand up by then."

That evening they had more delicious fresh bread, with their indistinguishable stew, and tins of applesauce from the cargo they had brought. Penny slept on her canvas cot as though she had been etherized.

Several more days of sweeping, scooping, scrubbing, and spraying were needed, and then they proceeded to whitewash the interior walls. Surprisingly, it looked almost decent. Smoke stains and streaks of black and brown from roof leaks were much reduced. The moment the whitewash dried, they could begin moving cots and equipment into the new wards, ready for patients to be moved from the overcrowded intake hospital.

And then Penny discovered what Jane and Frannie had been doing since they arrived.

She went to the hospital with them early in the morning, and immediately found herself surrounded by an appalling distortion of childhood. These new orphans had been taken up from the streets of Alexandropol and Erevan, or found lying at their gates, barely moving. Emaciated, fragile, wasted. Exhaustion was written on every face, their eyes dull and unfocused. And the filth all over their bodies was a palpable presence.

"I can hardly believe they are alive," Penny whispered to Jane.

"These are the lucky ones who were brought in with some hope of recovery," Jane told her. She set Penny to work on the bathing team, the first essential step in the intake process. Since the weather was still warm enough, this work took place outdoors in a courtyard.

Most of the little ones were nearly naked, and the few shredded garments some of them wore were removed by women with rolled-up sleeves and placed using pitchforks directly into a fire. Water was poured again and again over the children to loosen the dirt, and then they were lathered up and rinsed. Penny watched the other workers and tried to do exactly what they did.

"Sorry," she said to one of them in Armenian. "I can't find any soap."

"Right here," the woman answered. "In this pail." A bucket beside her was full of a grayish clay, semi-liquid, like mud. Seeing Penny's confusion, the woman told her, "It's bentonite. It comes from the hills near here. Very good for washing."

And sure enough, the slippery substance had just enough grit in it to remove the dirt and dreck from the little bodies.

The children went immediately from the bath to the barber, who cut and shaved off all of the hair on their heads. At this point it was clear that most of them were covered in skin and scalp lesions, angry red sores on their arms and legs, and yellowish crusty blisters on their heads. So the next step was a soak in a sulfur bath. Metal tubs were set up in a row across the courtyard—with sad, motionless, little bald children sitting in them. Penny remembered bathing her younger siblings and their joyful playing in the water, which sometimes got out of hand. But these poor little girls sat in silence, meekly accepting anything that was done to them.

One of the workers, a friendly young Armenian woman called Alma, showed Penny how to recognize the presence of scabies in the skin. "It's not just a sore, it's a parasite," Alma explained. "A tiny mite that burrows into the skin. You see the red bumps here, in the hollows of the knees and elbows, often on the wrists. Almost all of them have it, and it passes from one child to another. But if we are very firm with it right from the start, within three days of treatment it is usually controlled. See, you need to do this."

Alma rubbed some translucent ointment from a big glass jar into the skin of a little naked child standing on a crate. "Sulfur ointment," she said. "This is six percent sulfur in petrolatum. But of course it is very greasy and rubs off easily, so then you must cover it with cotton." A great heap of clean flour sacks cut into wide strips lay on a table beside them. Alma wrapped these bandages around the child's knees and arms, expertly knotting and trimming the cotton strips with a pair of scissors hanging from her waist. "You need to carry scissors at all times," she said a bit reprovingly. "Ask at medical inventory. And you must never lay them down anywhere, not even for a moment."

Penny smeared petrolatum while Alma wrapped the bandages, for what seemed like a very long time. "That's good," said Alma at last. "You have a sharp eye. Now you learn the next step."

After the children were washed, barbered and treated for scabies, they got their scalp inspections. Many of their little heads were covered with crusts and ridges in a distinctive circular pattern, like rings of blisters. "Favus," said Alma. "That's the name of this nasty thing. It's a contagious condition as well, caused by a fungus. Not easy to treat, but we are having some success. In the villages, they used to spread tar on the child's head and then rip it off. The blisters and the hair would come off with it. It works, but *so* painful—who wants to do that to a child? We use this instead," she said, wielding a huge purple bottle. "Tincture of iodine. You put it on a rag like this," she said, demonstrating. "Then soak it into the sores. Sometimes it hurts them, but not like the tar treatment."

The child they were working on did not even flinch. Penny was taken aback by their depression, their weariness. Each child just stared into the distance, passive and still.

"The iodine we do for a few days, till it starts to look better. Then we use pine resin salve—very sticky, and smelly, too. But it smells better than the blisters. I think they smell like mouse droppings."

"Whatever they smell like, it isn't very nice," said Penny.

"We make cotton kerchiefs to wrap their heads, to cover the pine resin. You'll see."

"Can you tell me . . . what causes their bloated bodies? They are so terribly thin, yet their stomachs are swollen up like a balloon."

"We call that 'hunger belly.' It comes from eating things they cannot digest, with no protein or food value. They try to eat grass, clay, tree bark . . . a plant called *lebeda* that seems like food but it only makes them sick." They continued dabbing the heads of the children with iodine.

"Alma, thank you for teaching me. You're very kind."

"I have learned it all from Dr. Artine. He is wonderful. Thank God for him. He is our general surgeon, and they all say he is brilliant. From Western Armenia. He went to the Syrian Protestant College to study medicine, and because of the deportations he is here."

"Did you come here that way, too?"

"No, I am from Erevan. I have been working to help the refugees since they began to come here, almost four years ago." Alma paused. "Very hard work," she said in a low voice.

"*Dzerk it talar*," said Penny, using an Armenian idiom. *May your hand be always productive, like an evergreen.* Hearing this, Alma stopped short, then unexpectedly gave Penny a brief, firm hug.

For the next stage of Penny's training, Alma handed her over to Jane Eberlee.

Jane was working in the inner courtyard of the complex, where about three hundred children all sat, silent and apathetic, on the ground. An assembly line of medical care was set up along the walls. Several nurses and helpers gathered around tables holding medical supplies: bottles of sterile water, tubs of disinfectant for the women to clean their hands between patients, trays of small mysterious tools and implements. A line of about twenty children at a time submitted themselves to trachoma care at this station.

"Welcome to our eye clinic," said Jane with an edge of sarcasm. "This is the most serious condition that we treat daily—trachoma, a contagious disease of the eyes that can cause blindness. So many of them have it! And it spreads so easily! We really need to isolate these cases in a trachoma hospital. Miss Finn and Dr. Ruhl are working to get one established at Seversky Post, and it can't happen a moment too soon."

Penny observed the stages of this process. First, a helper swabbed a child's eyes with absorbent cotton, using boiled water with a little boric acid added to it. This dissolved any solid discharge, sometimes heavy enough to coat the child's eyelids and lashes.

The child moved on to the next position, where one helper held the eyelids open and another gushed liquid into the eye using a glass rubber-bulb pipette with a smooth, pointed nozzle. "Is that boric acid, too?" Penny asked.

"No . . . it's a fairly strong solution of silver nitrate, two to four percent. It should destroy or at least reduce the microorganisms that cause this disease. I'm sure I don't have to remind you how important it is to disinfect your hands thoroughly, over and over again. And if the pipette touches the eye, then it must be sterilized as well."

But there was more to come. At the next station, a nurse sat in a straight-backed wooden chair, and the child was made to kneel on the ground facing away from the nurse. The child's head was tipped way back until she was gazing straight up at the sky, and the nurse pinned the child's head between her knees. "This step is more difficult and requires two skilled practitioners," said Jane. "You see, this disease is so dangerous because of the granulations that develop on the inside of the eyelids. Can you see that? Here, use my magnifying glass. They look like little grains of bulgur wheat soaked in water. If they are not removed, they will rub over the cornea every time the patient blinks an eye. It's the constant scraping that damages the cornea, leaving many little abrasions on it, until the surface becomes cloudy and the patient can't see anymore. Without treatment, blindness is almost inevitable."

Penny was becoming very tense at this point. There was something so intrusive about poking around on the inside of someone's eyes. Everyone else seemed quite calm, even the child whose head was trapped between the nurse's knees.

"So, one person everts the eyelid—that is, turns it inside out—using this little disposable bit of wood, like a matchstick. You grab the eyelid and turn it back over the stick, as if you were rolling up a window shade. Then the seated nurse scrapes the inside of the eyelid with one of these copper tools. Copper has antiseptic qualities, you know, and the tool is very smooth, so it can remove the granulations without damaging the inside of the eye."

Penny found that she could not even watch this procedure being done. "Maybe I could help with the washing stage," she said anxiously. "Over there, at the beginning."

"Oh certainly, they all need irrigation. Never enough hands for this job. And the active cases need treating every day, until the granulations disappear. Even after that point it may still be communicable. Hence the need for isolation."

"Yes, right. Whatever you say," Penny agreed.

She was put to work irrigating eyes with silver nitrate solution, while Jane returned to the last point in the process, at which she inspected every patient thoroughly to judge the progress of the disease. Jane had a box filled with charts for each child, where she and a helper made detailed notes.

Penny was able to squirt liquid into each eye, with another person holding the lids open and catching the runoff in a kidney-shaped enameled basin. But she still felt disgusted—even frightened—by this whole process.

She did her best, patient after patient, even though the woman working with her seemed a bit rough in her handling of the children. It reminded Penny of the way she might handle meat in the kitchen. A couple of times, Penny nearly said something about it to her, but then realized that this worker had probably been at it for a long time already and knew what she was doing. The children failed to react to it at all.

A child came into their hands whose eyes were swollen nearly shut; the woman forced one of the eyes open, and the child cringed. Careful to say nothing, Penny began to wash out the eye with silver nitrate solution. But then she realized that the eye was somehow alive—the mass of material inside the eye was not only pus, but a nest of little colorless worms.

With a gasp, Penny stepped back and dropped the glass pipette upon the ground, where it shattered. The woman frowned and made an exasperated noise.

"Ja-a-a-a-a-ne?" Penny's voice rose, high and shrill. "I mean, Doctor Eberlee? Could you come here for a moment, please?"

Jane Eberlee moved down to Penny's station and peered at the eye with her magnifier. "Oh yes . . . we see this nearly every day. It happens when the child has been too weak to brush away the black flies, and they lay their eggs inside the eyelids. Before long, you have a pretty foul mess. This will be a case for Doctor Ruhl, the eye surgeon. He'll have to do a lateral canthotomy to open the lids . . . he'll make an incision here, with the patient under anaesthesia of course, and then peel back the tissue and clean all that out. It's a fairly routine procedure."

Jane glanced up at Penny then, and saw the girl with her eyes squeezed tightly shut, shaking her head fiercely, waving her open hands in front of her face as though she were fending off a cloud of black flies. "Ohhhh," said Dr. Eberlee. "Well . . . eye surgery is not for everyone, you know. I'm sorry about that."

Penny could barely speak. "I can manage swarms of roaches. All right? I can manage scrubbing off dirt and—and excrement. I can cope with skin and scalp diseases. But I cannot . . . cannot . . . maggots in a baby's eyes!"

"I'm thinking it's about time for a break. Why don't you go take a walk for a bit? A long walk."

Penny left the clinic and walked quickly away toward the outer perimeter of the compound, a very large space several square miles in its area. She passed numerous stone buildings in various stages of disrepair, some with no roof at all, and just gaping holes where doors and windows used to be.

She kept walking, on and on, whispering quietly, as she did back in Oberlin when everything became a bit too much for her. She was angry with herself, and ashamed.

At length she came round to the great Orthodox church on the site, built by Tsar Nicholas for his regiments, dedicated to Saint Arsenius. It had been reconsecrated as an Armenian Orthodox church, and the distinctive Russian crosses were replaced by Armenian ones. In the weeks since they had arrived at Kazachi Post, she had never been inside. Because she was not Orthodox, she was afraid it might give offense, and she was not sure what the protocol for solitary female visitors might be. But today, her heart drew her irresistibly inside.

The space was huge, cavernous, with an enormously high ceiling; small windows well up in the two towers sent dusty shafts of light down onto the bare floor. Hundreds of the Tsar's soldiers could worship in there at a time. There was no furniture at all, except for a table near the entrance where a few tall thin tapers showed a flicker of light. The larger windows along the ground level were closed by heavy wooden shutters.

She tried to imagine what it had once looked like inside, in its heyday, glowing with golden-framed icons and perhaps rich carpets or hangings. It was now stony, dark, almost empty, but somehow beautiful that way. A few icons hung at the front of the sanctuary, with candles burning before them in small glass bowls of red and gold. A feeling of spiritual power lingered in the air like incense.

She knew that services were conducted there; the *badarak* or Divine Liturgy was sung every day by one of the two Gregorian priests who were employed to offer it. She thought she spotted one of them in the shadows. He might have appeared when she entered to see who was there. Self-consciously, she pulled out a white cotton handkerchief from her pocket and draped it over her head. When she was a child in Tabriz, her Armenian nannies and girl friends had always covered their heads in a church. The priest did not confront her, and apparently withdrew.

She raised her hands, palms open, and shaped words silently with her lips, pouring out all of the disorientation and fatigue and inadequacy she was feeling.

Dear Father, I don't really know why you have brought me here. Everyone else seems to simply do what needs to be done, better than I can. Of what use is my presence here? I do not understand what you are asking of me. I am eating food that someone else might need. I am taking up space. But what am I giving? How am I helping, in any way that a refugee woman being paid in corn grits could not do instead?

She continued to pray in that quiet darkened sanctuary, until she became aware of some other people arriving and moving around. Perhaps it was nearly time for a worship service to begin. Putting her handkerchief back in her pocket, she slipped away.

That evening, after a mostly silent supper with the other tired staff workers, she returned to the intake hospital to see how the children were doing, the ones she had washed and treated during the day. The little ones—three, four and five years old—had been fed a proper hot meal with sweetened condensed milk, and placed into the first safe and clean beds they had known in a very long time. These were merely army cots covered with a cotton quilt, and there were four small children to every cot. Two heads on one end, and two on the other, with all of their little feet in between. But it was a vast improvement over their desperate, hungry, scared existence surviving on the street, searching for food and shelter.

Two women working on the wards during the night moved in and out of the room. A kerosene lamp burned all night, up high on a shelf, providing just a faint but comforting light. Penny walked quietly up and down the rows of beds, studying the sleeping faces.

As she passed, one of the little girls stirred, her face scrunched up in distress, reaching out her hands into the air. A bad memory? A nightmare? Penny went to her and crouched down on the floor beside the cot. She lay a hand upon the child's chest and patted her; she stroked the arms and face lightly. The child was barely awake and did not look at her.

Searching her mind, Penny found an Armenian lullaby her nannies used to sing to the children in her family, back in Tabriz. At first she hummed the melody, then the words came back to her, and she began to sing, very softly.

> *Koun yeghir palas, atchert khoup ara*
> *Nakhshoun achkeroud koun togh ka vera*
> *Oror im palas, oror ou nani*
> *Im anoushigees kouneh ge dani.*
> *Doun al koun yeghir, indzi al koun dour*
> *Sourp Asdvadzamayer anoushees koun dour.*

> *Go to sleep my dear, close your eyes*
> *Let sleep rest upon your pretty eyes*
> *Lullaby my dear, lullaby and sleep*
> *Sleep takes my sweet one.*
> *Go to sleep now, and grant me sleep as well*
> *Holy Mother of God, grant my sweet one sleep.*

As she sang, the child she was touching began to relax. But then other heads were raised around her, as at some level of consciousness other children heard the song and responded. They listened. Some opened their eyes, then closed them again. They settled their heads back down on their cots, and snuggled close to each other. Small ripples of contentment passed among them. It was not Penny to whom they were reacting, but to some deep level of memory or experience they loved and longed for.

On the following night, Penny moved her own army cot into the intake ward and slept there. And whenever a small sound or movement disturbed her, she went to the restless child, touched her gently, and sang.

Chapter 4

It was at about that point that Penny recognized what might have been obvious to her from the start. The children had almost no clothing. And certainly not what they would need when the weather turned cold and harsh, which it already showed some signs of becoming.

The children in the hospital area wore nothing but underwear, which made sense while their skin and scalp were undergoing treatment.

But she began to spend time with the older girls, aged six and up, and discovered that they too were very much in need of proper clothing. They had some shapeless garments, hastily sewn, that offered no protection from the elements. No warm sweaters, no stockings, no shoes.

She went to talk to her friend Alma at the intake clinic.

"Alma, we need to find these children better clothing. What can we do about this?"

"The whole nation of Armenia needs better clothing. Don't you see that? Clothes items are more valuable than money, by far. People will kill you on the street to steal your hat or trousers. It's so hard to find any yard goods to make clothing . . . our cotton crop has gone unsown for several years now. One can't eat cotton, you know. And all of the sheep were made into meat, so there is no wool. Very expensive and dangerous to travel into Persia or across the mountains to buy goods. We keep asking the N.E.R. to bring us old clothing from America, and they say they will try, but they have to fill their ships with corn and wheat right now, so we are still waiting."

"I thought we brought clothing bundles in the *Hamilton* from America . . . I remember masses of clothing in the warehouse. Where is it now?"

"How can I know? I only know that we need it."

Penny thought it was time to go and search the storerooms near the train tracks. When she got there, she found Mr. Yarrow and Mr. Costen engrossed in conversation, so she waited for them to finish. They were going over inventory lists on clipboards with deep concentration and some concern.

Ernest Yarrow was making another quick visit to Kazachi Post to assess their food needs and prepare for the next shipment; he did not look happy at all.

There was a pause in their negotiations, and Yarrow noticed Penny Prior standing there waiting. "Yes, Miss Prior? What is it?"

"Sorry to interrupt you. I just came to ask if some clothing bundles could be brought here. And about any sewing supplies we might have available. The children are not well dressed for the fall weather."

"No, they are not, and it's certainly time we addressed that. Miss Prior, I expected you to apply yourself to this problem before now."

Penny looked at him, startled. "I don't understand, Mr. Yarrow . . . what am I to do? I have nothing to address it with, so far as I know."

"What about the yard goods and sewing machines we brought in the last shipment? And the used-clothing bundles? What have you done with them?"

She was completely at a loss. "Well, I don't know. I haven't even seen them."

She noticed a look of chagrin on Mr. Costen's face. "Let me help you with that, Miss Prior . . . we'll be finished here in a moment," he said.

Penny moved some paces away to wait for them. Finally, Mr. Yarrow walked off, apparently not very pleased with either of them.

"Miss Prior," Costen began, "I do apologize for this. It's really my fault. You didn't deserve that. We've been so overwhelmed with trying to organize the storage here . . . we've been scrambling ever since we arrived, and we are shorthanded, you know."

"Yes, of course," she said, still mystified.

"Please come with me. I'll show you where the clothing and other stuff is stored." He guided her through the storage area to a locked room at the end of the primary magazine, found the right key, and opened it for her.

When her eyes became adjusted to the dim light, she saw that there were great heaps of tightly bundled old clothes in the room. A stack of fabric bolts lay covered with an oilcloth. And against one wall stood several small wooden crates, still sealed.

"I kept intending to bring you ladies here to hand over all of this. What with the food and construction gear and medical supplies, I just let it slip. Please forgive me."

As her mind took in the potential for all of these goods, she felt renewed, elated. "Oh, this is wonderful. Wonderful! Thank you!"

He glanced at her doubtfully, still expecting an angry reaction from her. "Ummm . . . that's great, I'm glad. Just tell me where you want it delivered, and I'll organize a corn team to bring it all to you." They used the term *corn team* for groups of hired laborers paid with rations of corn grits.

"Let me organize some space first . . . somehow."

"Yes, sure. Listen, I have to say . . . Mr. Whitney, you know, was our senior inventory manager, the real logistics expert. Shears and I have been trying to learn it on the job, so to speak. I think I really dropped the ball on this, and I'm sorry. Also, please don't blame Mr. Yarrow either. He's feeling a lot of pressure right now . . . some of the other stations are running short, and he was here looking for any supplies we could spare for them. I suppose it annoyed him that we have stuff here we haven't even used yet."

"Never mind, Mr. Costen," she said. "I don't think I could have managed it before this, anyway. I've been too busy with other things, too. And I didn't even realize that Mr. Yarrow was expecting me to do this."

"We're all doing our best under tough conditions," Costen said.

Penny went as soon as she could to Sahag Asdourian, the Armenian instructor who had led their language training on the sea voyage out. He was now in charge of education for the girls at Kazachi Post. Several volunteers had been giving the girls some lessons before this, mainly to keep the children busy during the day, but they were not professional teachers. He was facing the challenge of teaching children from preschool to young teens, with very little in terms of instructional resources.

He and Mr. Arnaud were working on setting up a couple of large buildings for classrooms and workshops, including a textbook printing office. She found both men directing a cleaning and refurbishing team, and she raised her pressing issue with them.

"We need a large space—perhaps more than one—to set up an organized clothing factory here. The children are urgently in need of winter clothes, and one could regard it as part of their vocational training as well. I want to teach as many as I can to knit, to sew, and to alter or re-tailor clothing. What can you do for me?" she asked boldly.

"I think we can provide two large rooms," said Mr. Asdourian. "But they are quite empty. We have no desks, no tables, not even chairs. Can you work like that?"

"We shall have to make do," Penny answered. "There is always the floor."

"The floor we have ever with us," said Arnaud.

As soon as she had keys to two large empty rooms, she went back to Mr. Costen and had all of the clothing bundles and supplies brought over from the magazine. To her surprise and delight, she found that the small wooden crates contained twelve brand-new Singer sewing machines, all of them hand-powered. The corn team helped her to set up a reasonably workable space: an ample area for unpacking and sorting the used clothing bundles, two rows of Singer machines standing on their crates, and another open area for laying out and cutting fabric.

She also found a small parcel containing the all-important tools of the trade: scissors, measuring tapes, pins and needles, and a quantity of thread. Not enough, but it was a start.

There was one keen disappointment, however—the bolts of fabric they had brought were wholly inadequate. Thin, skimpy cottons, more suitable for tea towels than clothing. They would do for a hospital gown or nightshirt, perhaps a chemise or a pair of bloomers, but only that. Probably they had been purchased by some man who knew nothing about sewing. She would need much more fabric of a sturdy and adaptable kind.

One evening at dinner she spoke about this lack with Jane Eberlee. "Well, you know," said Jane, "We brought the whole contents of a field hospital with us. There must be a sizable stock of sheets in there. We never use sheets in the clinic—the children have no concept of them. They are accustomed to sleeping on quilts, and under quilts, but cotton sheets are only a hindrance for us."

"Really?" Penny said, her voice rising with excitement. "Bedsheets! Heavy, strong cotton. And hospital sheets too, intended to stand up to boiling and bleaching. That would be just the thing!"

"Come with me tomorrow and we'll see Miss Dirouhi at the medical inventory room."

They did go the next day to find Miss Dirouhi, and Penny nearly wept to see stack after stack of new, crisp, folded hospital sheets. "Thank you, Lord," she said aloud. Miss Dirouhi and Dr. Eberlee glanced at each other and smiled.

The plan developed by Mr. Asdourian called for a half day of class-room teaching for the children and a half day of vocational training and institutional chores—cleaning, laundry, cooking, scrubbing, caring for younger girls—and now, sewing. They were to divide the census in two, with half in the classroom in the morning and on the job in the afternoon, then switching, to maximize the use of space and staff. Mr. Asdourian was already preparing teachers for the classroom work, and it was up to Penny to find squads of girls ready to learn to sew.

She already knew many of the girls aged ten and up. Before long she had enlisted morning and afternoon groups of girls eager to have some-thing to occupy their minds and hands.

The day she introduced them to the clothing bundles was a memorable one. They were as excited as a Christmas morning, unfastening the bundles and laying out great spreads of donated clothes. The idea was to sort it into piles of children's clothing that could be used as is, adult garments made of fabric that could be reused, and unsuitable items that could be sold in the towns in exchange for additional thread and other supplies.

But in no time, it turned into a free-for-all of trying on all sorts of silly items, the more inappropriate the better. There were frilly nightgowns, absurd hats, impractical shoes. They were all overcome with laughter, so rowdy that Mr. Asdourian came to see what was going on.

He and Penny both laughed with them, gratified to see signs of healthy childhood in these youngsters at last.

She had taught her younger sister Matilda everything she could about tailoring and dressmaking, just as her dear Auntie Nan had taught her, back in Tabriz when she was ten and eleven years old. She had taught groups of girls at the Collegiate Presbyterian Church sewing club in Oberlin. She knew how to break down the procedures into comprehensible parts, assign specific tasks to those able to accept them, and direct the process toward attainable goals.

Among the clothing they found, incongruously, a whole bundle of old umbrellas. That caused another outbreak of hilarity. But Penny began to think seriously about how to adapt them for reuse. They carefully detached the water-resistant cloth from the umbrellas and turned it into small rain ponchos for the children. Then, Penny disassembled the metal ribs, and discovered that with only slight modification they could be used as knit-ting needles. A knitting team was recruited to create as many small warm stockings as they possibly could, and to begin learning how to knit vests and sweaters as well. Old garments were unraveled and knitted into new ones.

Before long, they were turning out a steady product line of recaptured clothing. But the real mass-production effort went into sewing the hospital sheets into simple, functional, proper garments for growing girls. Penny designed a one-piece dress with half-sleeves and a fitted buttoned waist, reaching to the knees; she created patterns or muslins in a range of sizes, using the flimsy bolt cottons, and teams of girls cut out these pieces while others learned to operate the Singer machines. She had no trouble enlisting older girls—aged twelve through fifteen—to manufacture the finished dresses. The older girls became assistant teachers as well, helping the younger ones acquire each necessary skill.

Soon, she was able to send a report to Mr. Yarrow detailing the number of garments they had produced, requesting many more bundles of used clothing and shoes, and appealing for more hospital sheets.

Penny made another visit to the St. Arsenius church to give thanks.

"If I may say so," Arnaud told her one night at dinner, "You seem like a different person lately. Have you discovered a secret stash of strawberries somewhere? Or maybe a lovely roast chicken? It would be awfully unkind of you to keep it to yourself."

"I'm afraid not," she replied. "Nothing but this . . . stew. I'm telling you, canned chipped beef is getting very monotonous. It's like cans of dog food."

"At least it's not dog *meat*," said Arnaud.

"Or so they say," Penny noted. "To answer your implied question, I'm just feeling as if I have settled in better now. Found some work I can really do. And how I *love* being so close to the girls, as they are learning and sewing together. Feeling very thankful."

"Happy to hear that."

"I scarcely dare to ask . . . but how are things going with you-know-who?"

"Sahag Asdourian? He's a perfect peach."

"Oh stop—you know what I'm asking. How are you and my father getting along? Is he learning to use the new press?"

"In a word, no. He has absolutely no interest in the Gestetner. Considers it an accursed innovation. Even though it's working pretty well now to produce classroom materials. Would you like to come by and see it?"

"Oh, of course. Please, show me."

A day or two later she went to the newly-established printing office in an upstairs classroom, where somehow they had managed to scrounge a table and a couple of chairs. On the tabletop stood the printing device, under its solid, glossy wooden cover. Arnaud unlocked and lifted off the cover to reveal the very modern-looking apparatus inside.

There was an impressive metal frame, black and shiny, with a central mechanism and two big black rollers operated by belts. A large chrome hand-crank extended from one side. It had gears with teeth and small steel knobs for making adjustments, the uses of which she could not imagine. Beautifully scrolled silver trim and an official plaque enhanced its appearance.

"It's properly called a Cyclograph, in fact, though everyone refers to it by the name of its inventor. A huge step forward in office automation. You see, before this press came along, copies of important documents had to be written out by hand—contracts, deeds, wills, accounts, all sorts of legal writ. Like poor old Bob Cratchit was doing in *A Christmas Carol* . . ."

"Bartleby, the Scrivener!" Penny interjected.

"Sorry?"

"Oh, that's just something I read in school. A story by Melville."

"Right . . . as I was saying, after all this laborious hand-copying, every page had to be minutely examined to ensure they were identical, as human error generally bollocksed it up to some degree. Beg your pardon, Penny."

She merely gave him a tolerant look.

"But now one can cut a stencil with this fancy little stylus, and attach the stencil to one of these drums. Ink is applied here—just the right amount—and the pressure rollers spread it evenly and force it through the tiny perforations in the stencil. Then a sheet of paper is fed in here, and the ink on the drum is transferred to the paper, more or less intact. It takes some practice to get it right, without smearing or leaving faint empty spaces. But now we can run off this immortal literature with some degree of efficiency."

He showed her a printed sheet containing letters of the Armenian alphabet. Beside each letter was a cunning little illustration, of the *A is for apple* variety. There were drawings of a sun, a key, a hat, a flag, a bell, a hen, a fish, a butterfly. "Why, this is lovely," she said. "The pictures, they are so charming. And the letters—like works of art. Like the large illuminated letters in a beautiful old Bible."

"Mmmm," he said diffidently. "Not sure they merit that kind of praise. But I have to approach the whole project as a drawing challenge, since I can't really read Armenian. Sahag tells me what he wants depicted, and gives me a model letter to imitate. It's an elegant language, visually, though still mostly meaningless to me."

"I wonder, though . . . what about the older children? Beyond the alphabet stage?"

"So astute, my young friend. You have already put your finger on the weakness of our system. I brought two typewriters, but only for the English alphabet. And it seems that our chance of obtaining an Armenian-alphabet typewriter is essentially nil. Writing out lessons by hand with a stylus is possible, but I don't think I will ever be able to do it. Sahag is trying, but he's not very handy. Your father could probably do it. But I believe that too is unlikely. The stylus is tricky to work with, for those who are not artistically inclined . . . a typewriter to cut the stencils would be much easier to use."

"Well, that's very frustrating."

"Agreed. A trip to Erevan or Tiflis to see whether we can barter some secondhand clothes for someone's office typewriter may yield results. And for publishing proper textbooks, we need a printing press."

That would have been the exact moment for Gordon Prior to walk through the door, but it did not happen that way. Instead, he found Penny later in the sewing rooms.

"Penelope, you need to begin packing for our trip to Tabriz. I have heard from the American Consul there, a Mr. Danforth, and he has given us permission to come."

"What? A trip to Tabriz?" It seemed people were forever springing surprises on her.

"Yes, we need to go and collect my printing press. Mr. Danforth confirms that it's still in good order."

"But . . . how can I leave the sewing classes? We have only just got them well underway."

"You'll need to find a substitute teacher for two or three weeks."

Easy for you to say, Penny thought. After working on it in her mind for a while, she went to see Miss Dirouhi at the intake hospital, and then her friend Alma, asking them if Alma could be permitted to oversee the sewing classes in Penny's absence. There was some resistance to leaving the hospital short of one skilled staff member. Penny promised to be back as soon as possible.

She did not even ask her father why it was so essential for her to go with him. She already knew that it would be her job to buy train tickets, negotiate with food vendors and tea sellers, look after his accommodation, and so on . . . all of the tasks he considered to be beneath his dignity.

Penny sensed that Gordon Prior was disappointed to find himself living in the staff quarters at Kazachi Post, bunking with other men, instead of in the kind of exemplary missionary home his wife Wellandette had established for them in Tabriz. Penny was only too glad; she was able to have her separate life at the Post, and not devote herself to the Reverend Prior's housekeeping. He still regarded her in a proprietary manner, nevertheless.

Following Mr. Yarrow's instructions, each of them packed their Sam Browne belts and service revolvers, even though both of them had only the vaguest idea how to use a gun in self-defense.

On the day of departure, Mr. Costen gave them a ride to the train station at Alexandropol in one of the Ford trucks. Penny went inside to buy their tickets.

When the train was ready for boarding—a passenger train this time, with actual coaches instead of boxcars—she found that the stationmaster had automatically sold her first-class tickets. The Priors had their own compartment with two berths.

The once-elegant train had seen some rough days during the war. Tattered velvet curtains hung at the window, and the leather seats were now cracked and peeling. But one could still see the embossed letters S-J-D on the headrests, for *Sakavkasnaja Jelesnaja Doroga*, the Trans-Caucasian Railway. Centered at Tiflis, the railway was a relic of the European pretensions of Georgian society in the pre-war era.

The train journey went fairly smoothly, considering. It was indeed an advantage to have Penny's native fluency and natural habit of treating Armenians as her peer group instead of as Oriental underlings. Gordon Prior alone would have found it a much more disagreeable trip.

They had arranged to make one stop before moving on to Tabriz: at Echmiadzin, the seat of the Patriarch of the Armenian Apostolic Church. At the ancient monastery there, Catholicos Gevorg the Fifth presided over a church tested by fire.

The monks were said to operate the only movable-type printing press in all of Armenia, and Gordon Prior was keen to see it.

The venerable buildings of the monastic compound were very much in need of repair, the great trees all cut down for fuel, the study rooms and quiet retreats of the monks now packed full of homeless refugees. The Catholicos received them in a large but sparsely-furnished visiting hall in his former patriarchal palace, in which he now occupied a single modest room.

Unexpectedly, there was another foreign visitor present: an Anglican clergyman called Bassgarden. Apparently he was attached to the office of the Catholicos in some semi-official capacity, representing the Lord Mayor's Fund and its charitable outreach in Georgia and Armenia. Bassgarden seemed cordial and approachable, if a bit superior in his attitude.

"We are here to extend assistance to the Orthodox, you know, as members of the great liturgical brotherhood of faith," Bassgarden announced. "I understand that the Near East Relief is a secular organization with a very high concentration of Protestants."

"I would not call it 'secular' so much as 'non-sectarian,'" replied Reverend Prior. "But our aid is available to all, without regard to confession or affiliation."

"Yes, quite," said Bassgarden, not clarifying whether he considered that a good thing or a bad thing.

The Catholicos proved to be a gentle and restrained elderly person, bowed down by much grief. He said little during their interview, which took place in English. They were served small glasses of tea.

"The situation here in Echmiadzin has improved somewhat, since last winter," Bassgarden was saying. "The Turks came within five miles of Erevan, you know. On the open plain between this city and Mount Ararat, over two hundred thousand refugees encamped. The church and the people here had to provide for them somehow, while having little to sustain themselves. As many as a thousand died in a single day."

"Delighted to hear that there has been some improvement," murmured Gordon.

"Oh yes. In fact, I was thinking of moving north, to the Alexandropol area, myself. Could perhaps offer a boost at your barracks facility there. Dab hand at administration."

"I believe we are a bit understaffed in some areas. We lost our primary inventory manager in a tragic accident at Constantinople."

"Ever so sorry to hear that. Perhaps we can look into the possibilities."

"For now, I'd like to have a quick look at the printing operation here."

"Yes, so I've been told."

"Not much time before our train departs again, so . . ."

The Catholicos himself intervened at this point. "We use the press to print our precious Scriptures and service books. Many were lost in the war. Also lost were the brothers who operated the press. And now we are not sure whether it is still usable."

They trooped off to the printing room, where Gordon cast a critical eye on the old but apparently quite solid machine. He quickly touched several of its key parts with a trained hand.

"It appears to me, sir, that the machine is sound and functional, with the exception of this rusted clamp," Gordon said to the Catholicos. "I am on my way to Tabriz now to fetch my own Armenian printing press. I probably have a spare clamp among the parts I intend to bring back."

"You can repair it?" said the elderly gentleman.

"Looks like it, yes. Let me stop here again on our return trip, and I'll try and set it to rights."

"That would be a great help to us, good brother. We should be ever in your debt."

"So, do you by any chance have an Armenian typewriter you could spare?" asked Penny.

The men all stared at her as if a dog or a cat had suddenly entered their conversation.

"Don't think so, young lady," said Bassgarden. "Things are still written out the old-fashioned way here, for the most part."

They soon took their leave and got back on the train, which was lying over on a sidetrack for servicing. After another hour or so, its steam had gathered again, and they resumed their journey.

And although Penny had resisted leaving her own work behind, as they grew closer to the Persian border, she became more and more excited. Back to Tabriz! Her own home town! Her mind went over all of the places and people she still held dear from her childhood. She wondered whether any of them could still be found there.

At the border, Persian gendarmes boarded the train to inspect their papers and baggage. The border was a fairly porous one and these formalities did not take long.

They received a warm welcome from the American Consul, Lewis Danforth, and were assigned two comfortable guest rooms for their use. Penny could not believe that she was about to sleep in a bed with a mattress and sheets and a counterpane, for the first time since they had sailed from New York.

Danforth was indeed very kind during their visit, providing the use of a small carriage and a driver. They went all over the town looking at the things they remembered: the Protestant Armenian church there, the two large Mission schools, the Citadel, the gardens, the ruined Blue Mosque, and especially, the wonderful medieval covered bazaar. As they walked the narrow vaulted pedestrian lanes of the bazaar, the sights, the sounds, the smells were all overwhelming for her, and tears streamed down her cheeks. Even the merchants who would normally try to badger a visitor into buying their goods stepped back, seeing her emotion, feeling a natural compassion for it. Her heart was filled to bursting with love for Persia.

War damage in Tabriz turned out to be minimal. There had been a great deal of political and social upheaval, but not so much of the physical kind.

But their home—the house she was born in, where she had lived until age eleven—proved to be an exception. Danforth told them that it had been sealed and guarded until 1917, but at that point the United States had entered the war as Turkey's antagonist, and their neutrality expired. In the disorder that followed, looters had found the house a tempting target.

The little carriage dropped Penny at the house, while Gordon went on to the print shop to examine the press.

Here was the walled garden where she and her sister and brothers had played. It was quite bare now except for a few date-palm trees. A small fountain was empty and broken, with many of its ceramic tiles fallen away, like a mouth with missing teeth.

Inside, she found wreckage everywhere, thick with dust. All items of value had been carried off, or destroyed in the attempt.

She moved quietly from room to room. Here was the day nursery, where the nannies looked after them. Here was the night nursery. The beds had been removed, but she could see them in her mind: here, she slept with her sister Matilda; there, her brother James slept; there, her youngest brothers, Max and Wallace. And there, the night nurse who kept them from disturbing their mother.

Here was the dining room, with the long table where her Auntie Nan had taught her to sew. Their Singer machine had of course disappeared. Auntie Nan—Annalisa Graybill—was Mrs. Prior's sister, and had also served as a missionary in Persia, at the Fiske Seminary school for girls near Urmia. Nan was Wellandette's opposite in almost every way: affectionate, competent, selfless, and devoted to the work of the Mission. She had escaped in 1917 to Buraan with the little girls belonging to the boarding school, and several of their dedicated Assyrian teachers. And now, Penny had a message from Nan, in her own voice.

She brought out of her pocket a letter that was handed to her by Mr. Danforth as soon as they arrived in Tabriz. It had been in his possession for some time, waiting for her. Standing in that empty, ransacked house, she slowly read it again.

> *My precious Penelope,*
>
> *How joyful I am to learn that you are returning to our region, and now as a member of the Near East Relief! The little girl I taught to sew buttonholes is now going forth into the world to help others. May God be praised for this glorious gift.*
>
> *I am sending letters to various places where I think you may alight on your way, in hope that at least one will turn up in the same place and time as you. This letter can travel through Mr. Patterson's consular system to Tabriz, and I will send likewise to Tiflis and other destinations.*
>
> *You are likely aware that when I fled from Urmia with all of the children from the Fiske School, in 1917, we ended up here in Buraan. The American Mission has been most hospitable to us, and all of our girls and teachers have found a haven here—with the exception of three dear little girls who did not survive the journey.*
>
> *In addition, the American Consul from Urmia arrived here in November 1918 just after the Armistice, and we were married in the Adamu Presbyterian Church by the Rev. David Galloway. My beloved husband Charles has been an inexpressible blessing to me, such as I never expected to find. My heart glows with a deep joy.*
>
> *Darling Penny, I hope you will stay well and be strengthened and enabled to carry on with your valuable work, no matter what you may encounter. I certainly discovered reserves within myself that I very much needed, in order to cope with the chaos in Azianlu during the war. You too will face challenges. Keep a level head and trust in God.*
>
> *I imagine that it has not been easy growing up in your household. Remember that I have been dealing with your mother and father much longer than you have. Perhaps living with difficult people has prepared you for trials yet to come.*
>
> *I only wish Charles and I could be there to meet you in Tabriz, even if I had to drive a Russian army truck the whole way! But that cannot happen, as I believe I am now carrying his child. No more adventures for me. It's your turn now!*

*May our Lord protect you every moment and grant you every
grace you need.
Sending you my greatest and tenderest love . . .
Your Auntie Nan (Mrs. Charles G. Patterson)*

Penny pressed this letter to her breast and wept again. Too many waves of memory, too many tempests of emotion, too many wise and loving words.

She knew that the carriage driver would soon be back to collect her, so she took one last walk through the house. This time she noticed something she had missed before—on the floor, in a few broken pieces, lay a saucer from Welly Prior's wedding china.

The wedding china! There it was, again! Penny picked up the pieces and fitted them together, then laughed aloud. *Oh Mother, here is what is left of your everlasting wedding china.*

The carriage brought her to the sizable brick annex behind the Mission school for boys where Gordon Prior had done his printing work for the Armenian Protestant churches and schools of northern Persia. She found him inside, looking like the cat that had swallowed the canary.

"Ah, Penelope," he said, smiling. "Come and see what we've got here." It took her a few minutes to understand what she was looking at. The massive iron press took up the center of the large room; the huge heavy thing was of little use to a casual looter, and they could not even find a way to vandalize it, so it stood nearly untouched. Loose paper and other rubbish was strewn about in their search for something valuable to steal.

But then she realized that parts of the wooden floor had been taken up, revealing hidden storage space underneath. And that space was filled with tray after tray of tiny lead type, still perfectly in order, ready to be used.

"Your father was not caught flat-footed by the outbreak of war. Not he!" said Gordon Prior, speaking of himself grandly in the third person. "Ohhh no . . . I suspected that we might need to depart in short order, so I had these concealed spaces built, to hide these precious fonts. All it would take is a thoughtless vandal tossing them on the floor to render them nearly useless. So when we were preparing to leave, I hid them all down under the floor . . . and here they are."

Penelope was impressed. She looked at her father with a new respect.

"And look at this, too . . . copies of all of the Armenian-language textbooks we created for the schools here. Language texts in Armenian and English, mathematics, history, science, literature, rhetoric, geography, Bible studies and religious education. We kept copies of everything we produced, of course. No need to start from scratch . . . we can recreate these materials for the children of Armenia."

"That's brilliant . . . it's really wonderful. I'm so proud of you," she heard herself saying.

"Mr. Danforth has offered us the use of a heavy Reo truck to carry it all back to the Post. Plus a driver, and a couple of armed guards to protect us. It's helpful to have certain personal and professional connections," he said smugly. "I can't wait to see Asdourian's face when we show him all of this." *And Arnaud's too*, thought Penny. *But that's all right* . . . Reverend Prior deserved credit for his achievement, this time.

The trays of lead type were carefully wrapped and loaded with the press and the books in the back of the Reo truck. Penny added a large parcel of thread and other sewing supplies she had purchased at the bazaar. They made their farewells to the excellent Mr. Danforth and promised to come back to visit when they could.

On their way back to the Post, they stopped by the monastery at Echmiadzin, and Gordon Prior was able to replace the rusted-over clamp on their printing press with a new one. He also agreed to receive any monks the Catholicos wished to send to Kazachi Post to be trained in the use of a moveable-type bookpress. Prior welcomed the additional manpower that such trainees would provide.

But Penny also learned to her dismay that Bassgarden had invited himself to travel with them. "Have you found yourself an Armenian typewriter yet, young lady?" he asked in his patronizing way. She ended up spending the rest of their journey sitting in the back of the Reo truck with the Persian guards, who spoke no Armenian. Yet the trip to Tabriz, she had to admit, had been a resounding success.

CHAPTER 5

THE sewing factory was now going so well that they were able to make garments for the boys' orphanage at Polygon. In return, the boys repaired and remade a steady stream of shoes for Kazachi Post at their leathercraft workshop.

The engineering team of Franklin, Brownlea, and Merle had accomplished a great deal on both posts. They had installed many more water heaters and better laundry facilities, expanded and upgraded the kitchens, set up generators for some electric light, and replaced panes of glass in dormitory windows to make the rooms warmer in the increasingly chilly nights. They had worked out how to use the cheap, crude *mazout* oil that could be brought there from Baku, so they did not have to rely on scarce wood or imported fuel.

The boys' orphanage too instituted the half-day system of schoolwork alternating with vocational training. Workshops were gradually taking shape for them to learn carpentry, ceramics, and metalwork; they showed keen interest in acquiring skills that would make it possible for them to survive in Armenia's economy once they had aged out of the orphanages.

Improving facilities meant constant pressure to increase their census of resident orphans. Thousands of needy children still haunted the streets of every Armenian city. They lined up, cold and hungry, in front of the gates of every shelter. As soon as the shelters could accept more, those places were filled.

Dr. Eberlee and Dr. Artine led assessment teams that ventured into the towns of Alexandropol and Erevan twice a week to collect children to admit to Kazachi Post. They could select only as many as could be processed at the intake hospital, where each group required intensive treatment before they could be moved into the general orphanage population.

One day in mid-October, Jane Eberlee told Penny that she was in a bit of a bind, as her primary medical interpreter could not accompany her on their planned orphan-harvesting trip into Erevan that night.

"What's wrong?" Penny asked. "Is she ill?"

"No, it's a family emergency of some kind. She'll be gone for several days. I wish I could speak Armenian better—I just haven't had the time to work on it."

"Of course you haven't. Jane, let me go with you."

"I . . . I hesitate to ask this of you, Penny. I know you found the work at the intake hospital to be . . . upsetting. To be honest, the condition of the children on the streets is far worse. What we must do is this. We must differentiate among three groups of children: those who are well enough to continue surviving on their own for the time being, those who are in a perilous state but may recover with treatment, and those who are dying. We can admit only the second group. That means saying no to scores of children who plead with us to shelter them. It's soul-crushing work . . . I don't know how to hide that fact."

There was a silence. "All right . . . I know I'm not very good at steeling myself against a situation like that. It's true. Pretty sure I could not do it on a regular basis. But you are in a fix right now, and I want to help you."

Jane sighed. "I'm going to ask you to forgive me in advance."

"I just hope I won't have to ask *you* to forgive *me*," Penny replied.

They traveled into Erevan in one of the Ford trucks, with two Armenian guards and a hospital nurse. It was an early autumn dusk when they arrived, and getting dark quickly.

"Why do you come and do this at night?" Penny asked. "Wouldn't it be easier in the daytime?"

"At night we can tell better which children have no shelter. Many children are out on the streets in the daytime and then go to something resembling a home and a family at night. The ones who are still out on the street after dark are the ones with nowhere else to go."

The truck moved very slowly through the narrow streets. Penny saw a corner with five children scattered around on the pavement, separately. Two of them were sprawled in bony heaps, apparently already dead. The others were sitting hopelessly or lying curled up against the cold, too weak to react at the presence of the truck.

A little further on lay a boy so emaciated that his arms and legs reminded Penny of chicken bones from which all the meat had been eaten.

His bare rib cage arced up over his collapsed body. Beside him sat crouched on the ground a ragged woman covering her face with a scrap of cloth, unable to watch her child die. She too was so sunken in anguish that the arrival of possible help meant nothing to her.

They drove to a more open area in front of a shuttered government building, where there was enough room for the truck. A small cluster of nearly-naked children waited for them, hoping that this would be a night when the truck would come. The guards established a perimeter and a sort of queue. Beyond this ring of minimal control, a pitiful crowd soon gathered, reaching out their hands and moaning, "*Haaaatz . . . haaaaatz.*" Bread . . . bread.

They placed a kerosene lamp upon a crate, and Jane Eberlee sat on a chair, with Penny standing behind her, translating her questions and statements into Armenian. The nurse selected children from the crowd and sent them to Jane, one by one.

Dr. Eberlee really needed nothing but her own eyes and fingers to assess the level of malnutrition of the children before her. When a child seemed comparatively well, she asked a few questions about where they spent the day and how they obtained food; some of them were able to get along on the rations provided at the N.E.R. soup kitchen near the train tracks. To those, she had to deny access to the orphanage, and then they had some heart-wrenching scenes of disappointment and pleading. Penny found herself telling these children, "Maybe next time," even though she suspected that she was holding out a false hope.

She tried to avoid eye contact with any of the distressed children. But then she realized that this served only herself, not them. After that, she made the effort to connect with them, to encourage them, to make sure they knew where in the city they could go for help.

It took a few hours to fill the back of the truck with thirty tattered, filthy, hungry children, most of them less than six years old. A thin wail went up from those left behind.

"Dear God in heaven," Penny whispered to Jane.

"Yes," replied Jane, grimly. "I'm sorry."

The next day, Penny looked closely at each of her sewing students, in their relative health and safety. The girls were properly dressed now, clean, fed, with bright eyes; even their shorn hair was growing out again. She embraced each of them like her own daughters. Surprised, some of them wriggled and giggled. Teachers did not normally behave like that. But many of the girls earnestly hugged her, too.

At that point in time, Penelope Prior was not even aware of one of the most dramatic episodes in the involvement of the Near East Relief in the Caucasus. It had taken place before she arrived, but it had a lasting impact on the way she was serving the children now.

This story began in the fall of 1917, when a young Presbyterian divinity student at McCormick Theological Seminary in Chicago, one John Elder, heard the call of the Y.M.C.A. for volunteers to travel to Russia to aid the war effort. Their somewhat naïve objective was to go and lift the spirits of the demoralized Russian soldiers holding the eastern front against the Germans and the Turks.

They decided that what the Russians really needed to hold their lines was some wholesome recreation, tea rooms, facilities to write and post their letters home, interesting lectures on science and art, musical evenings, and Protestant religious services.

Fifteen young Y.M.C.A. appointees left San Francisco on 11 October 1917 to sail to Japan, since sea travel across the Atlantic was far too dangerous. From Japan they traveled in winter weather for two weeks on the Trans-Siberian Railway to Moscow, and dropped right into a city in the rolling boil of an epic revolution.

The Russian Army did not have a lot of time for tea parties and science lectures. Factions of Tsarist loyalty and Bolshevik rebellion were in outright civil war within their ranks. The Germans were making gains on them from the west, and in the Caucasus the Ottoman troops were at their very doorstep. Russian soldiers were deserting the front, disbanding their units and shooting their officers. In this scene of chaos and mutiny, the Y.M.C.A. volunteers arrived in Tiflis in December 1917.

Elder and his colleagues were met by the American Consul in Tiflis, a man with the unforgettable name of Felix Octavius Willoughby Smith. Smith was not sure whether he was happy to see them or not. He was certainly in need of help to cope with the tide of Armenian refugees pouring into the Caucasus from eastern Anatolia, to whom he was channeling relief funds. On the other hand, here was a contingent of inexperienced young Americans to look after. He decided to send them on at once to the refugee relief operation in Erevan.

Perhaps it would be best to allow John Elder to tell the rest of this story in his own words.

31 December 1917

The American Consul in Tiflis, Mr. Smith, gave us a warm welcome, and tells us our help will be very much needed in Erevan. He says that perhaps we can help to buck up the Georgian and Armenian troops in the spring, as the Russians appear to be preoccupied for the time being. In the meanwhile, we are to help with the refugee relief.

7 January 1918

Have settled now in Erevan, and went round with Mr. Yarrow to see the relief work they are carrying on for the refugees. Countless families have turned up here after fleeing from Turkey. They are packed into every corner of every town in Armenia, plus those who are forced to camp in the countryside.

The method they employ to help them is splendid. Instead of giving simple handouts, they give employment to as many as possible, sewing clothing for the needy. Starting with the raw wool, they wash it, card it, spin the yarn, dye it and weave the cloth. Many mothers support whole families this way. The men are employed as carpenters and builders, road-work crews and sanitation helpers. Mr. Yarrow seems a very able leader.

20 January 1918

Had a nice visit with Aram Manougian, member of the Armenian government here. He says there should be work for us supporting their soldiers. Perhaps we need not abandon our original plan after all. He stipulated three conditions: no drinking, no gambling, and no political or religious propaganda. In view of our Y.M.C.A. affiliation the first two of these should of course pose no problem, but I am hopeful that Christian worship and fellowship will still be allowed.

26 January 1918

Met a General Silikyan today, who is eager to have us open a morale club for the Armenian soldiers. He has promised us a couple of rooms at the government center, ten pounds of sugar and five pounds of tea, a big samovar, and a movie viewing machine. Saw the rooms and they are great.

1 February 1918

Rooms coming along nicely. Got electricians in there to install outlets, lighting. Carpenters putting together tables and chairs. Plaster and white-wash nearly done. Saw the Erevan mayor, the chairman of the Armenian

Committee for Public Safety, the regimental commander and the chief of police. Invited them all to the official opening of our new "Y."

7 February 1918

Opening Day! It was a great success. Aram Manougian, General Silikyan and the mayor all came, plus other local dignitaries. Mr. Yarrow spoke some words of welcome, as did the head of the local hospital, a fine man whose proper name I did not quite catch, but everyone calls him Doctor Artine. There was a very nice party and we showed a short film called "Together at the Front." Glad we can carry on this ministry while also helping out with the refugees.

28 February 1918

In just our first month, we served over 21,000 cups of tea, gave 1,031 haircuts in the barber shop, and 564 men used the writing room for letters. We had non-denominational prayer services with hymn sings every Sunday and Wednesday evening. Thankful that the Lord is blessing our work.

My good friend James Arroll has the gift of relating to the soldiers and giving them encouragement. He speaks fairly fluent Russian.

4 March 1918

The news on the whole is not good. The Georgians and the Armenians in Tiflis are unable to cooperate, and both of them detest the Tatars in Azerbaijan. They are incapable of running a government together. Never mind fighting against the Turks. We hear that the Russian Army has fallen apart, in full retreat. Doing a lot of looting on their way. They are supposed to be our allies.

The men at the soldiers' "Y" are angry and anxious. They think the joint government will fail thanks to the deliberately obstructive Azerbaijani leaders.

7 March 1918

What has gotten into the Tatars? This morning fighting broke out in the city itself. People ran madly up the streets, shopkeepers pulled down their shutters, soldiers ran past us with guns, cavalry galloped around telling everyone to take cover, children cried and women screamed. James and I looked out from the balcony. A block away, soldiers were firing down into the Tatar quarter of the city. Why? Also we could hear gunfire on all the streets around us.

In the park behind the church, some Tatars and Armenian soldiers were wounded or killed. James and I went out to see if we could be of help. We saw Aram Manougian take a very daring chance and get away with it. Some 150 Tatars came up the street carrying one of their wounded in the direction of the hospital—a commander, perhaps. Manougian came into the street just at that moment. He was exposed to their fire . . . we all held our breath. But then he walked directly into the crowd of Tatars, shook hands with them, and accompanied them to the hospital. He delivered their wounded into the hands of our Dr. Artine. It was a bold move and served to bring some order back to the city.

14 March 1918

We have heard today the town of Erzurum has fallen to the Turks. That is only about 170 miles from here.

24 March 1918

News comes today that Petrograd and Odessa are in German hands and they are moving down toward Batoum. Armenia's forces are still falling back toward Kars. Consul Smith is very concerned . . . advises all U.S. citizens to leave at once, on a special train which may be the last. They are to go to Baku where there is still a British presence and escape from there.

With some difficulty got permission to stay for myself, James Arroll, and three members of the American Relief Admin group. The others all left, twenty-four of them, including Mr. Yarrow. A sinking feeling to see them depart. But for now we can carry on the both the "Y" work and the relief work. There are about 13,000 homeless orphans on our relief rolls, mostly housed in Armenian state orphanages, some in foster families. We call those "home orphans." Plus about four thousand spinning women making cloth and supporting several family members on their wages. Plus Dr. Artine's hospital. In all I believe we are supporting some 50,000 people every month. The A.R.A. supplies are getting much harder to obtain as we lose territory.

30 April 1918

Now Kars is to be surrendered. That is only 80 miles from here. They are reported moving toward Igdir, just south of Erevan. I would be willing to shoulder a musket myself for these people. I could shoot Turks who are trying to massacre Armenians with a conscience void of offense.

The post office refuses all mail, foreign or domestic. With no trains running either north or south, we feel very isolated.

5 May 1918

A last visit with Consul Smith and the A.R.A. men before they go. James Arroll and I insist on staying. There must be someone here to deliver the relief funds. Smith says he can still wire the money to us; he would stay and do it himself but he has official instructions to leave. When James and I heard that there are still funds available, that settled it for us. We are staying.

21 May 1918

Has the end come at last? Reportedly Igdir is in Turkish hands. They are only 25 miles away, a march of a day or two. Aram Manougian called me in privately and told us to leave. We have distributed almost all of our remaining food supplies and cloth to our local workers, but they are not authorized to handle American relief funds. So we shall stay.

Poor James is quite ill right now with a fever, so there is no possibility of our escaping anyway. I must stay close and care for him as best I can. Dr. Artine, bless his soul, has been here to visit him and says he cannot be moved.

I have written a farewell letter to my parents in case the worst shall come. Perhaps someone will send it after I am gone. I'm sure they never expected to lose their only son at the age of twenty-three.

26 May 1918

Well, you never can tell what may happen! Just as the end seems at hand, the pendulum swings the other way, and the Turk is in retreat!

General Nazarbekian reports that he has recaptured Karakalis. After a two-day battle at Sardarabad, the Turks have been completely routed. I don't quite understand how it has come to pass, except by the hand of God.

1 June 1918

We have obtained a money order for about 50,000 rubles. Immediately, we put a couple of thousand spinning women back to work. Food supplies are dropping fast. Now that the Turks are retreating, they are leaving nothing but scorched earth behind. Stealing all livestock, stores of harvested grain. Everything they cannot carry away is burned. I am shocked by the sheer barbarity of this behavior.

It seems that men at war behave either with conspicuous bravery and heroism, or with appalling cruelty. I suppose there is a group of average fellows in between, but nobody ever writes odes or histories about them. I think I must be firmly in that group.

22 July 1918
Today is my birthday. I have made it to the age of twenty-four after all.

11 August 1918
I had the honor of attending the opening session of the Parliament of the Republic of Armenia. Since the Trans-Caucasian Republic failed, each of the three national groups has had to cobble something together on their own. Georgia, Azerbaijan and Armenia will have to make a go of it as three separate states. They are like tiny fleas in the fur of Russia and of Turkey. But all we can do is hope for the best.

A free and independent Armenia for the first time in 600 years or more—that is something to celebrate! There was a great crowd present in the National Hall, and I offered congratulations on behalf of the United States of America, the Near East Relief, and the Y.M.C.A. Why not? I am all of that right now.

The band played the national anthem for each government represented, and it was hard to tell which was the Star-Spangled Banner and which the Marseillaise. Doesn't really matter since there are no French citizens here anyway, but they are our allies in the war.

Sadly, the Republic of Armenia has started out at a terribly difficult time. What with the war, thousands upon thousands of refugees, essentially no budget and most of their fit men still deployed, they have a very hard row to hoe. But here's wishing them well.

3 September 1918
Prices are skyrocketing. Food and other supplies are very scarce. The ruble is nearly worthless. I am taking on many more workers just to feed them, even though the looms are often idle because we cannot obtain any wool or cotton to make into cloth.

The fall harvest is turning into a dreadful failure, as the destroyed land yields nothing, and west of here in the breadbasket of Armenia, the Araxes Valley, the Turks are seizing tons of wheat, barley, rice, and grapes, sending it all back to their own people. Not a beast is to be seen on the farms these days . . . even the donkeys, dogs and cats are disappearing. We are receiving displaced persons in the hospital who are too weak to stand, so weak that they merely fade out of life. I am terrified for the coming winter.

James Arroll is still convalescing—that is to say, I hope he is convalescing, and not making a slow slide into oblivion. I can rarely find any digestible food that can sustain him.

28 October 1918

Hunger and disease are the masters of our world now. We are helpless before these ruthless forces.

Every day walking to work through the English Garden, I see dead or dying refugees. Even on the main streets they are dying, unattended. We have hired men to work on clearing bodies from the streets and a squad of grave-diggers to cover them. I have heard of a priest who conducted 33 funerals in one day, and then dropped dead himself at the end of it.

It is already painfully cold . . . the old men are predicting the harshest winter in many years, according to some kind of Poor Richard's Almanac type of indicators. That is exactly what we do not need. I have started praying shamelessly for mercy.

James Arroll is a bit better, though I cannot explain how. When he can travel I hope to evacuate him to Tiflis, where food supplies are said to be somewhat better.

19 November 1918

For weeks I have not gone to work without hearing the heartbreaking sobs of children, grimy, half-naked, freezing and starving by the wayside. The English Garden is now a wasteland of death. One constantly sees a two-wheeled cart pulled by a couple of men, into which wan parents place the still form of one who was once the joy and pride of their hearts. The cart rattles away, leaving behind desolate benumbed mothers who must face the bitter, weary, hungry days and nights ahead with aching hearts. There is no service and there are no mourners. Only silence and agony.

I can still receive funds from abroad, but of what use is it when there is nothing in the markets to buy?

The Armistice has been signed to end this war. I feel no joy and very little hope.

5 January 1919

For some weeks I have been alone here as I did manage to get James Arroll to Tiflis. I believe he will get better care there.

Sometimes I can find a source of food . . . I believe many speculators have hidden whatever supplies they have, as the prices continue to climb.

Once in a while I find someone who is ready to sell. I was told that the government has made it illegal to sell sausages or ground meat, for fear of secret cannibalism. This may be a malicious rumor, but it is quite plausible.

And the street children are still enduring it all. We opened another orphan shelter at Nova Bayazid with strict instructions for them to admit no more than 150 children. The director wires back to me that he has taken in 300 and has no food for them. Nor do I.

From Dilijan comes a cable, REFUGEES DYING OF COLD AND STARVATION SEND SUPPLIES AT ONCE. But I have no supplies for these distant places. I cannot even touch the desperate need right here.

In my heart is a great ache that hurts all the way through. Tears are always on my eyelids at the sight of the dirty, trembling, shriveled waifs lying about on the streets.

The adults are like walking trees without leaves. There are very few old people left.

In the countryside, people fare no better. Whole villages are reduced to empty shells, everything of value stripped away, the gaunt ruins of homes from which all scraps of wood have been torn out and used for fuel, leaving them standing open to the wind and snow and rain. The horseman of War has moved along, and now Famine stalks through this land. The degree of hunger is really beyond description. One man was found dead with a piece of his leather slipper in his mouth from which he was trying to get some nourishment.

Still we are responsible here in Erevan for idle factories on which 7500 people depend, orphanages with 1850 children, and a 120-bed hospital. The government operates many more facilities that are little more than storage units for dying children.

20 January 1919

There is some better news at last, but I hesitate even to believe it. I am told that the N.E.R. and the A.R.A. are now preparing large shipments of food aid for the Caucasus. A few ships are coming across the Atlantic now and they are trying their best to engage more of them.

23 February 1919

I am weeping with joy as I write this. James Arroll is back from Tiflis, where he was finally able to recover from his gastric misery. I scarcely realized how painful my loneliness has been until he returned. Thanks be to God.

The suffering I have been living through in these past few months has made me feel years older. It's hard to describe. I feel as though some large weight were tied to my head, pulling me down and down, until it seems that something inside me is bound to break.

2 March 1919

I believe we have crossed the great divide and the work will be getting easier from now on. The wheels of industry are slowly starting up again. A trainload of ground corn arrived yesterday, and another loaded with wheat flour is due shortly. The people are not familiar with corn meal and it would be better to have more wheat, but anything nutritious is so sorely needed.

I hear through organizational sources that the United States is now abundantly overstocked with certain commodities. They geared up production to feed the war effort and now there is a massive surplus, especially of corn. So we can expect to receive tons of corn meal, corn syrup and the like. We shall introduce a new menu to the Caucasus.

17 March 1919

A few days ago I went to Echmiadzin at the invitation of the Patriarch to see what we could do for their orphanages and refugee shelters. On the way we passed the carcass of a horse by the wayside. The smell of it was nauseating, yet we saw peasant women hunched over it tearing off small strips of flesh and consuming it on the spot.

At the cemetery they showed us that day's mass grave, prepared for about thirty distorted jumbles of bare bones that yesterday were living human beings.

I brought my camera along and took as many photos as I could, to document this calamity for the future. Those who have not seen it cannot imagine it, I am sure.

Many people are struggling to help others during this horror, but not all. We encountered an orphan who was badly burned . . . he had been begging at a home, and the woman living there had come forth in a rage and thrown a shovel-full of hot coals at him.

I don't know how much more of this I can stand. I have sympathized until my nerves are raw and there is nothing left in me but a mute resentment against the whole awful situation.

CHAPTER 5

11 April 1919

We estimate that there are about 200,000 people who must be kept alive until the next harvest and must receive a pound of bread or grits a day for the next few months.

The Minister of Refugees says that he believes 95 percent of those working for him are stealing supplies. In that respect we are lucky. We have some grand Christian men working for us. The Minister has asked us to take on more responsibilities, saying frankly that he trusts our men more than his.

Perhaps the proof of their faith in Christ is this: they are helping the A.R.A. to distribute food aid to the Moslems in Nakhichevan. We have received a florid letter of thanks from one Jaffar Guli Khan on behalf of their government. Our workers are now feeding these allies of the Turks. If they can do that, surely I can find some corner of compassion and forgiveness in my heart as well.

24 April 1919

New workers for the Near East Relief have arrived! There are now ten of us in Erevan! James and I are beyond the point of exhaustion . . . hoping we can leave soon. The new people must get their feet on the ground first.

I am traveling back from a trip to Alexandropol to secure permission to use some of the huge ruined Army barracks near there, for an orphan city. We want to start a colony of some eight thousand orphans on that site, and I have a hunch that General Silikyan will permit this. I traveled with our friend Dr. Artine to assess the potential for an orphan hospital or medical center there. If we are given the use of the barracks buildings, we will have to start the huge task of repairing and refurbishing them.

4 May 1919

The Armenian government has now turned over to us the care of all of their bankrupt orphanages, some 14,000 children residing in substandard facilities all over the country. We have officially been given control over the huge barracks complex at Kazachi Post, Seversky Post, and Polygon. The place is a mess and there are already more than 3000 children somehow camping there!

18 May 1919

There is good news, mixed with not-so-good news. Mr. Yarrow is back, on a recon mission to collect details of our staffing, facilities, and finances, to report back to New York. He has brought us letters from home!! After one year and 28 days with no contact with our families, suddenly to get several letters all at once made me so deliriously happy, I didn't know whether to shout, sing, laugh, or cry.

Unfortunately, though . . . I met Mr. Yarrow expecting to be able to resign and start for home at once. The war is over, we are dead tired, and I want to get back to my studies at McCormick. But Yarrow pleaded with us to stay long enough for the new workers who are due in the summer to get here. He is returning to the U.S. almost immediately to bring out the new people. I hope we can manage to hang on a little longer, or I shall die with my boots on.

22 June 1919

A.R.A. and N.E.R. provisions are now making their way into the country—not a flood, but a fairly steady trickle. So much more is needed. We are sharing the cost of refurbishing the Polygon and Kazachi complex with the Armenian government, since of course the buildings belong to them. Some progress is being made.

It is a thrill to see some of the skeletal little orphans begin to fatten up. Their ghastly faces, like skulls with skin stretched tight over them, are beginning to look like the faces of children again.

As they get healthier, they are beginning to learn to help with the house work, cooking, cleaning, washing and so on. This seems to be good for them physically and mentally.

27 June 1919

At last, I have my release. The new contingent of workers will embark in a few days and arrive later this summer. I have trained the other staff as well as I can to carry on the work. I should like to meet the new folk, but I am spent. James Arroll and I are more than ready to go.

Word of mouth has let people know that we are leaving . . . I have a whole trunk full of farewell gifts. At every visit I am presented with arms full of flowers, sweet little handmade tokens of affection, items of pottery, lovely quilts, specially embroidered *kosovorotka* shirts, of the kind that Tolstoy wore. How will those look back there in Chicago? The Government has given me a lovely engraved silver cup.

On Sunday morning as James and I finished our breakfast, we heard the sound of singing on the street outside, and went out to see two lines of girl orphans, holding flowers and green branches. They escorted us to the church, singing and cheering. On the way we were joined by many other orphans, most of whom would not be here today if God had not sent us to Armenia to help them.

On the steps of the church in the morning sunshine, there were more songs, farewell speeches, and more cheers as they all said good-bye. I was certainly proud of our wonderful Armenian family.

1 July 1919

In Tiflis at last, awaiting passage from Batoum. There is a slight chance that I may make it home before my twenty-fifth birthday.

CHAPTER 6

"I SWEAR by all that's holy, if that man comes into this shop again, I'll crush his head in the bookpress!" exclaimed Arnaud.

"You'll *what?*" Penny replied, alarmed.

"Oh all right, I shan't, if you insist," he sighed. "Perhaps I'll crush my own head instead."

Penny had come to the print shop for a word with her father, but ran into Bassgarden just as he was leaving. The man looked her up and down and passed by a little too close to her, as he was in the habit of doing.

"He was here bothering you, I suppose."

"As ever, yes," Arnaud muttered. "The man is a perfect bounder. Does no work himself, but constantly hovers about passing judgment on the way everyone else is doing theirs."

"I believe that's what he refers to as 'administration,'" said Penny dryly.

"Very shrewd indeed, my little friend. He devours our food, bunks in our billet, and is always underfoot except when there's work to be done. Then he's nowhere to be found."

"I wish we'd never allowed him to attach himself to us in Echmiadzin," Penny said. "He just clung on like a limpet, and Father and I didn't know how to get rid of him."

"I imagine the good monks there had seen through him long ago and perhaps encouraged him to move along. I know his type altogether too well. Comes on like a toff, but he's just as middle-class as I am. Probably the son of some village barrister, apprenticed to the local vicar, looking to snag a comfortable parish church in some respectable town. He's the sort who got a commission in the war on the strength of his plummy accent, just so he could have his own batman and never carry a pack. No use for his sort, obviously."

"How in the world did he end up here?"

"Oh, I imagine they just got sick of him at home, too, and sent him out as liaison to the Patriarch, which any silly old sod ought to be able to do."

"Well, it's also our fault that he knew we were short-handed at the Post," she said. "Father mentioned the loss of Mr. Whitney. So he sought out Mr. Costen and Mr. Shears and volunteered to take the night shifts at the warehouses. I don't blame them at all—I'm sure they were very glad to give up their twelve-hour shifts. I heard Bassgarden say that the 'natives' couldn't be trusted with the warehouse keys. But I understand from the Armenian staff that he has made himself a cozy little retreat over there, where he just sleeps the night away while they keep watch. That leaves him rested and ready to spend his days getting in our way over here."

"I'm sure he's writing long letters back to the Lord Mayor's Fund, telling them all about how indispensable he is to the care of the children in our orphanages. Probably some sly digs at the young and enthusiastic Americans who require the guidance of a mature gentleman like himself . . . exactly the kind of bosh that every degenerate old Englishman wants to hear."

Penny paused. "Arnaud, there's something else. I haven't told anyone about it, because perhaps it's my imagination or something." Her genuine discomfort made him more serious at once. "It's about . . . well . . . he often comes to the sewing rooms, and he pays no attention to me suggesting that he might be a distraction from our work . . . he watches the older girls in a way that . . . troubles me. Always trying to get close to them. I'm not sure what to do about it."

Arnaud looked at her as currents of anger and disgust passed over his face. "That bloody parasite," he said at last. "Perhaps it's not his head that I'll crush in the bookpress."

"Please, don't do something rash," she said. "It's just a feeling I have. I don't think he has done anything wrong."

"He *has* done something wrong," Arnaud asserted, "by making you feel that way. Young women have an acute sense of these things, I believe, through regrettable experience. If he does this again, let me know at once."

"Well . . . all right. I should be getting back there. I hesitate to leave them alone. Although some of the older girls have already been through so much—from men—during the war and deportations. They may be better equipped to deal with it than I am."

"All the more reason to protect them, at any cost."

"I agree. Is Father in the bindery? I just need to speak to him for a moment."

Penny found Gordon Prior working with the book-binding team, putting together the latest batch of classroom textbooks. "Ah, Penelope," he said. "Look at the fine work my class is doing. I've taught boys and men to perform this task, but I must say, these young women are among the best I've ever had. So meticulous, wonderful manual skills." He switched to Armenian to make sure the girls could understand him. "I tell you frankly, they are doing an excellent job. At least as good as any class I've ever taught." A number of bashful smiles appeared at this announcement.

"I am delighted to hear this. But not a bit surprised," Penny said, also in Armenian. She glanced around the room, catching the eye of each girl with an encouraging look.

"What can I do for you, my dear?"

"I came to ask whether you can spare two or three blank copybooks. I want to show the girls how to keep better records of our clothing production. Also, I'd like perhaps one more for myself."

"We can part with that many. But we have to be somewhat frugal with paper until the next shipment arrives."

"I'll be careful. You know we never waste anything."

On her way back through the print shop, she stopped for another word with Arnaud, who was engaged in printing Armenian language worksheets on the Cyclograph.

"Arnaud . . . you have done a lot of book illustration, isn't that right?"

"Oh yes. It's bread-and-butter work. The most lucrative thing I've done so far is color lithography for an edition of *The Boy's Camelot*. You know, that expurgated version of Malory's *Le Morte d'Arthur*. How boys do love all of that swordplay and jousting and armor and whatnot! Probably not much call for it here at the Post. But the audience at Polygon would enjoy it."

"Never mind . . . that sounds perfect."

"Perfect? For what, pray tell?"

"Oh, just a little idea I'm working on. See you later."

Arnaud promptly forgot this last exchange, as he prepared for another trip north to Tiflis. He had managed to find an Armenian-language typewriter there in reasonably good condition and paid for it with a man's woolen suit from the clothing bundles.

In the process, he became acquainted with a young man who worked as a contract employee of the N.E.R. at its orphanages there, teaching drawing classes. Arnaud thought teaching art could be another way to enrich instruction at Kazachi Post and Polygon, and might uncover some talent among their students and a new option for vocational training.

The scarcity of paper was a problem, however. They used every bit, including packing material and wrappers, sometimes laboriously steaming the crumpled sheets to flatten them. They constantly requested more paper in their freight shipments. He intended on this trip to buy some if possible, as the drawing master in Tiflis knew of a fairly reliable source.

The trip by train meant chugging across the Armenian plateau and climbing into the rugged mountains of Georgia, their crests already freshly decked with snow. The late autumn landscape was impressive but bleak, many of the towns and villages still only shells of privation and ruin. Georgia had fared better than Armenia in the war and received fewer refugees. The city of Tiflis, metropolitan center of the Caucasus region, still wore the faux-Parisian style of Imperial Russia like a faded frock. But there was hunger there, too, and much bitterness, and people looked ahead to another hard winter with misgivings.

Arnaud found the drawing master in his little flat at the top of a former office building, pressed into service as housing. It was just one small room, with a toilet downstairs in the courtyard and a pitcher and basin to wash in. Arnaud didn't care at all. "Orbeliani?" he called quietly at the door. The drawing master heard it and let him in. The two men embraced with the fervor of a new love.

They had become lovers from the moment they met, as if they had been searching for one another for years.

The days they spent together at Tiflis were brief and precious. Sometimes they used Orbeliani's little gas ring to heat soup and stay in. Often they went to small obscure cafes where they were welcomed, where they could drink and smoke and eat omelets and relax. They both knew how to be discreet and deflect any scrutiny from neighbors or employers.

Arnaud attended the orphanage drawing classes with Orbeliani and picked up some ideas about teaching art, which he had never done before. Some of the best students in the classes were young girls. Their teacher was a man of few words, but he was able to suggest just enough to the students to kindle their creative ideas. Then, he could work on improving their technique and draftsmanship.

Arnaud also discovered that Orbeliani had been assigned by the Near East Relief to take custody of a collection of medieval manuscripts, which were offered to them for sale. Trading with secondhand clothes and sacks of flour, they had bought several thousand parchment books and loose sheets of Bibles and liturgical works, saving them from loss or destruction. The manuscripts were to become the property of the Georgian government when their museums and libraries were functional again; in the meantime, they were stored securely, and two elderly scholars were employed to organize them.

"Georgie," said Arnaud one evening, "I've got to get back, you know. Time's up for now."

"Come back soon," Orbeliani replied.

"I'll try. Don't worry, I'll find a way."

They parted reluctantly, and Arnaud returned with a nice stack of wrapped paper and a set of oil pastels to Kazachi Post.

With Arnaud's return, winter arrived as well. Every puddle, every pail, every cup of standing water froze solid. Snow whipped into blinding waves in the air. The broad plain around the Posts became a flat white, the sky a dull gray; the world as far as the eye could see was suddenly colorless, featureless and cold.

The orphan rescue effort shifted into high gear, even though they had already been working hard; more helpers were hired, more buildings reclaimed. They burned through their carefully-managed supplies even faster than before. Children who could survive on the streets in the summer or fall with meals from the soup kitchens could no longer do so. The cold was sharp enough to kill.

The sewing factory at Kazachi Post expanded and intensified, with the urgent need for warm clothing. They worked as many hours as they had daylight enough to see, adapting and re-tailoring; the little knitters were turning out warm stockings, mittens, and vests just as fast as they could. It was tedious, repetitive work.

As the hours and days and weeks went by, Penny observed that her sewing squads were faithful to their task, but their energy began to flag. Their eyes lost focus, they sighed, they stared. They had to stop frequently to warm their stiff fingers above the little kerosene stoves that Rufus Kendrick had cobbled together for them from the tin cans that condensed milk came in. Penny delivered as much positive reinforcement as she had to give. And then she decided to follow through on the idea that had been developing in her mind for some time.

After her long days in the sewing rooms, she stayed awake working by the faint light of the lamp in the intake hospital night nursery, where she still kept her own army cot. Of the favorite books she had brought in her trunk from Ohio, she chose first *The Blue Fairy Book*. She filled pages of one of the blank copybooks with tiny handwriting in Armenian. She was careful to use every bit of each page of paper.

When it was ready, she brought the copybook with her to the hand-finishing room of the clothing factory, where girls of about ten through fourteen did the skilled fitting and basting of altered garments, while girls about seven through ten did the simpler work of sewing on buttons and hemming. The sorting, cutting, and machine-sewing rooms tended to be rather noisy, but this room was almost unnaturally quiet.

Penny looked around at all of the dark-haired heads, bent over their work. She stopped to assist a few students who were having trouble with a task. Then, she opened her copybook and began to read aloud.

"There was once upon a time a widow who had two daughters." Heads were raised, and eyes opened wide. Penny's naturally soft voice could be heard in the room, as it seemed every girl held her breath and listened.

"The elder daughter was like her mother in face and humor, both of them so disagreeable and proud that there was no living with them. The younger was the picture of her father in courtesy and sweetness, and likewise one of the most beautiful girls ever seen. As people often cleave to their own likeness, the mother doted on her elder daughter, and had an aversion to the younger, making her eat in the kitchen and work for them continually like a servant."

Penny had chosen the shortest and simplest story in the book, *Toads and Diamonds,* to begin with as an experiment.

"Among her tasks, this poor girl had to go twice a day to a spring two miles away to draw water and carry back the heavy clay jug to their house. One day, as she arrived at the fountain, she found a ragged old woman there, who begged her for a drink.

"'Aye, with all my heart, good neighbor,' said the kind young girl, rinsing the pitcher and taking water from the clearest part of the fountain. She held up the pitcher for her that she might drink the easier.

"'You are so kind and mannerly, my dear, that I must give you a gift,' said the old woman, who was in fact a powerful fairy who had taken on this disguise to test the girl's civility. 'At every word you speak, there shall come out of your mouth either a flower or a jewel.'

"When the girl reached the house, her mother slapped her for staying so long at the fountain. 'I beg your pardon for not making more haste,' said the poor girl. And in speaking these words, there dropped from her lips two scented roses, three pearls, and two diamonds."

Penny had the undivided attention of every child in the room. She felt confident that her Armenian translation was working. But alas, the girls were not. They had stopped sewing in mid-stitch and were hanging on her every word. Penny realized that she would need to address that problem later.

"'What is this I see?' said the mother, quite astonished. 'Pearls and diamonds come out of your mouth! How happens this, my child?' This was the first time the wicked woman had ever called her 'my child.' The girl related the incident at the well, while dropping out infinite numbers of sweet flowers and sparkling gems.

"'Come hither and see what comes out of your sister's mouth when she speaks!' said the mother to the elder girl. 'You too must have such a gift. You need only go draw water at the fountain, and when a poor woman asks you to drink, give her water very civilly.'

"'As if I should go to draw water like this common drab,' replied the wicked sister. Her greedy mother forced her to go, taking with her their best silver tankard. As the girl came to the fountain, out of the wood stepped a grand lady gloriously dressed. The same fairy was testing this girl to see how far her conceit and rudeness would go. She asked the girl to give her a drink.

"'Am I come hither to serve you, pray?' said the girl in her proud, saucy manner. 'Am I your ladyship's servant? Draw water yourself, if you've a mind to.'

"The great fairy said in her cool voice, 'Since you are so full of ugly words and so disobliging, I give you the gift that at every arrogant word you speak, out of your mouth shall come forth a serpent or a toad.'"

The listening girls sucked in their breath and looked quickly at one another.

"'Mother, your foolish plan came to naught!' cried the girl upon returning home, and from her mouth dropped a viper and two loathsome toads.

"'What evil is this?' the mother shrieked. 'It is that wretch your sister who has done this! And she shall pay for it!' The woman proceeded to beat the poor innocent girl until she ran from the house and hid herself deep in the wood. The king's son, returning from the hunt, found the girl helpless and alone, and desired that she should tell him how it happened to be so. And as she told him the story, she showered him with blossoms and precious jewels. The prince considered that she was lovely to look upon, and that such a gift was worth more than any dowry, so he conducted her to the palace of his father the king and there married her.

"Because the wicked girl made herself so odious with her snakes and toads everywhere, her own mother turned her out of the house, and she wandered about for a long while without finding anyone to take her in; she went to a far corner of the wood and there died."

The girls stared at Penny for a moment, and then they all began to react.

"They were half-orphans. Their father was dead."

"And their mother was selfish and cruel."

"She turned them out of their home. And the younger daughter was taken in, but the elder daughter found no one to shelter her."

"The younger daughter was kind to the needy woman. Even though nobody was ever kind to *her*. That is not an easy thing to do," said a thoughtful child named Katarine.

"I wonder though, of what use to her was that gift?" objected Maritza, a very intelligent and serious girl of fourteen. She was one of Penny's most able assistants in teaching and helping the younger girls. "It seems to me that she had no desire for flowers and diamonds. They simply made her valuable to other people. Like that lucky prince. Suddenly he got a beautiful wife who was a source of endless riches. What did he do to deserve that? And did she even want to marry him at all?"

A girl called Yester replied, "It's better than starving in the forest, isn't it?"

This vigorous discussion went on, as the girls brought up aspects of the story that Penny had never even thought about. She saw the spark of life returning to her dear girls in a way that moved her deeply. With a lump in her throat, she promised them another story tomorrow.

When the sewing class began the next day, the girls were all ready for it. She made them commit to keep sewing while they listened, so that the necessary work would get done.

"Once upon a time there was a poor farmer who had many children and little to give them in the way of food or clothing . . ." She had chosen one of her own favorite stories, *East of the Sun and West of the Moon*. This time, the girls did not wait until the end of the story to respond, but kept up a running commentary while Penny read.

"That girl's idiot father *sold* her to a *bear*," said Maritza bitterly.

"She wasn't an orphan, but perhaps it would have been better if she had been," agreed a girl called Rosa.

"She betrayed the bear who was really a prince. She disobeyed him by lighting the candle in the night. Maybe she shouldn't have been allowed to marry him," said Perouz.

"But she did earn him back by making that very long and dangerous journey. She made up for her mistake," added Nivart.

"That journey, though," said Veronika. "I'm not sure why it had to be repeated so much. All those witches, and the golden gifts, and the horses, and the winds. It went on and on."

"I like that," Nivart countered. "It's like listening to Bible stories in church. The same things are said over and over until you remember them. It's nice."

"That troll princess, she was something. The trolls were keeping the Christian folk as prisoners to serve them. Dirty people, who couldn't even wash a shirt."

"It was a magic shirt, Mina. With magic wax on it."

Penny was careful never to stifle their thinking with her own answers or interpretations. She simply read the text and let them take it wherever their minds should go.

The next day, she chose another of her personal favorites, *The Princess on the Glass Hill.*

"Oh, I like Cinderlad," sighed Altoun, age thirteen. "He's so brave, and clever. And though he seems rough and poor on the outside, underneath his tattered cloak he is wearing armor of gold!"

"Again, it's the youngest child who wins it all," Maritza grumbled. "Why? Often it's the oldest who does the most work in the family."

"The princess threw him the three golden apples, Maritza," said little Badaskan, age eleven. "I think that means she liked him and wanted to marry him. You're always talking about how the girl doesn't get to choose."

"Did she choose to sit up there on that glass hill in the first place? Sounds like it was her father's idea."

"Oh, there is something wrong with every story in your opinion, Maritza."

Very soon, the news got about that in the hand-finishing room the sewing class was having a wonderful new experience. Girls clamored to be admitted to the class. But Penny knew she had to keep the room small enough for her voice to be heard as she read. She had a negotiation session with the sewing class, and enlisted their cooperation in spreading the stories to the rest of the orphanage population. Each of them was to repeat the stories to others, and ask them to pass it along. Soon, over meals and in the dormitories and workshops and kitchens, stories were being told and retold, often with some original embellishments.

Arnaud addressed her one night over dinner. "Penny, I understand that Kazachi Post now has a thriving literary society," he said. "Sahag Asdourian tells me that the girls have a whole new interest in reading."

Penny smiled shyly but with great pleasure. "You know, Arnaud, you could help us if you want to," she said.

"Me? How? It seems you're doing a brilliant job all by yourself."

"Suppose we had some lovely color illustrations that we could put up in the sewing room. And perhaps in other places as well, the dining hall and so on. Pictures showing the people and the creatures in the book. Wouldn't that be nice? It could help the girls tell these stories to others."

"By Jove, that's an idea," said Arnaud, smiling. "I could do you something at least as good as those old Ford and Hood pictures. Perhaps an Arthur Rackham style. I have this new set of oil pastels I got from—that is, I got in Tiflis. Let me work up something for you."

"Oh yes, please. Oh, they will love it. I'm sure you know the stories."

"Let me see your copy for a refresher . . . if you have finished translating."

"I'm working well ahead. You can have it for a few days."

"That's all I need. I think some general pre-Raphaelite chivalric figures should suit."

"I think so. But don't forget the villains and the monsters."

"Goodness no, that's the best part."

Arnaud produced some wonderful pictures for her—bold knights in armor, graceful damsels in flowing apparel, scary witches and gloomy dark forests. The girls in the sewing room gazed at them in awe.

Penny was unsure about some of the stories in the book, ancient European race memories involving famine, murder, cannibalism, and very bad parenting. But she decided to carry on with the stories and see what the girls did with them.

"Long ago there dwelt on the edge of a forest a poor woodcutter with his wife and two children. The boy was called Hansel and the girl Gretel. And a great famine struck the land, so that he could not even provide their daily bread. One night, as he was tossing about in bed, full of cares and woe, he sighed to his wife, 'What's to become of us? How are we to support my poor children?' And their step-mother said, 'Husband, tomorrow we shall take them out into the thickest part of the wood; there we shall light a fire for them and give them each a last bit of bread; then we shall go away and leave them. They shan't be able to find their way home, and we shall be rid of them.' But the woodcutter said, 'How could I find it in my heart to leave my poor children alone in the wood? The wild beasts would soon come and tear them to pieces.' 'You fool!' said she, 'then we must all four die of hunger. You may as well go and plane the boards for our coffins.'"

"She wants to turn out the children in a famine so she doesn't have to feed them. That's just what people do," Rosa snapped.

"But of course they do," said Mina harshly. "When they are hungry, each one cares only about their own belly. Never mind about their children."

"The woman is not their mother. She's their step-mother."

"Sometimes, a step-mother might care for children much better than their mother ever did," Perouz replied.

"It was Hansel's cleverness that saved them. The adults were of no help to them at all. The children had to look out for themselves."

"But it was Gretel who burned up the old witch in the oven. She was just as bold and clever as her brother," Badaskan pointed out.

"The old witch pretended to be their friend, but she only wanted to fatten them up and eat them!" Veronika said with horror.

"What I don't understand is why they went back to their father's house after they were turned away to die. Just keep walking, you foolish children! What's the matter with you?" added Rosa in a heated tone.

After this, Penny was not eager to read similar stories, such as *Little Thumb*, with its fierce child-eating ogre. She tried some of the tales set in the Near East, such as *Aladdin and the Wonderful Lamp*. They did not care much for that convoluted story, though Arnaud's drawing of the magical genie made a fine impression.

They were more interested in *Ali Baba and the Forty Thieves*, and the resourceful slave woman Morgiana.

"Now she was a hero! She saved her master and the whole household. Twice!"

"But she was a ruthless killer as well. Don't you see that?"

"Sometimes it's a matter of 'kill or be killed.' That's the way the world is."

"But it shouldn't be like that. It's wrong. I liked the story of the girl with the glass shoes, who forgave her wicked sisters in the end. Even though they didn't deserve it," offered kindly Katarine.

"All of those thieves hiding inside oil jars . . . we have story like that, too. I remember it. From my village at Lake Sevan," said Yester, a forthright child of twelve. "Sevana Lich is high in the mountains, perfectly blue and crystal clear, and very cold all the year round," she went on, slipping into the ritual story-telling manner Penny used while reading to them. "The clouds pass over the lake and change its color to every possible shade of blue. And in the lake live the trout called *ishkhan*, the 'prince fish,' called thus because they have a row of spots like a crown around their heads.

"And on a rocky island in the midst of the lake is an ancient monastery, where some very old monks still live. And they tell of a time when the island was a refuge for the Christians against the attacks of the Turks. On one occasion a Turk, pretending to befriend them, asked permission to store his wealth inside the thick and high walls of the monastery. Thinking he was their friend, the monks gave him permission, and he ordered to be brought over in boats forty large crates of his supposed valuables, but inside each crate was concealed an armed soldier.

"And on that very day, one of the young novices of the monastery misbehaved, and as a punishment he was sent to sit alone in the dark storeroom. While in there he was startled to hear the sound of men's voices coming from the packing crates! He went to report this to his superiors, and the forty cases were promptly brought forth and pitched over the walls and into the icy waters of the deep blue lake! And that is what happened at the place of my birth," Yester finished, beaming with pride.

Again, Penny was overcome with tenderness for her lovely girls, and thankful for the power of stories to unlock their thoughts, memories, and feelings.

She began to suspect that *The Blue Fairy Book* had been exhausted for the time being, so she made a lateral move to a classic children's novel: *The Princess and the Goblin* by George MacDonald. She found that the girls loved the more sustained narrative of a chapter book, as well as the cliffhanger endings of each part, waiting eagerly for the next day's portion. Arnaud was put to work drawing the Goblin Queen and her stone shoes, as well as little Princess Irene and brave Curdie, the miner's boy.

"Now in these subterranean caverns lived a strange race of beings, known as goblins, who were not ugly in an ordinary fashion, but absolutely hideous, grotesque in both face and form. They chose living away from the sun, in cold and wet and dark places. Over many years they grew in cunning and they grew in mischief, and their great delight was in every way they could think of to annoy the sun-people who lived in the open air above them. They sought to torment them in ways that were as odd as their inventors; and they had strength equal to their cunning. In the process of time they got a king and a government of their own, whose chief business was to devise trouble for their human neighbors."

"There, you see?" cried Mina. "The goblins are just a lot of Turks."

"No, Mina!" replied Perouz. "There are many kind and good Turks. It's not fair to make them all the same. Some of them sheltered us children during the war, when our own parents could not."

Altoun spoke up again. "Curdie is the brightest and bravest boy of all. I love the way he makes up rhymes to upset the goblins, and stomps on their squishy feet! After all, those goblins shut him up in the rocks to starve. And they wanted to kidnap the Princess and force her to marry their horrible Goblin Prince."

"Princess Irene is eight years old . . . just like me," said a child called Lusia. "And she has a lovely, lovely great-grandmother."

"She's almost an orphan, since her mother is dead and her father lives far away. Only a *myrig* to look after her," said another child, applying the Armenian word used in the orphanage for their care assistants.

The story continued until Curdie overheard the goblins planning to dismember him and feed his body to their animals, and then there was a small mutiny among Penny's audience. She laid the book aside for a few days, and then asked them if they wanted to continue. The vote was in favor, so she went on, but found herself trimming a bit of the goblins' cruelty, even though it was so clearly imaginary and exaggerated.

She told herself that perhaps it was time for more realistic fiction, with no fantastic monsters or terrible threats. And that is how she came to turn to Lucy Maud Montgomery's *Anne of Green Gables*.

Chapter 7

"Miss Cuthbert explained, 'Matthew drove the buggy over to the station at Bright River,'" Penny read. "'We're getting a little boy from the orphan asylum in Nova Scotia and he's coming on the train to-night. We've been thinking about it for some time—all winter, in fact. My brother Matthew is getting up in years, you know—he's sixty—and he isn't so spry as he once was. His heart troubles him a good deal. We sent word for them to choose for us a smart, likely boy of about ten or eleven. We decided that would be the best age—old enough to be of some use in doing chores right off and young enough to be trained up proper. He's coming on the five-thirty train and Matthew has gone to collect him.'"

"An orphan asylum. They asked for a child from an orphanage, and they are going to *send* him. To people he has never seen before!"

"Imagine how terrified he must be!"

"It's shameful. How can they *do* that?"

Mina said, "People come *here*, you know, and ask for girls of Maritza's age. They want a girl to keep their house and raise their children, just like a servant. We learn housework and child-minding here, so they think we are already trained. I heard this from Varvara in the office. But the people here won't do that."

"No, surely they won't! They are not going to give us away to just anyone!"

All of the girls in the room stared meaningfully at Penny. She kept her silence as usual, but on this occasion she did shake her head *No*, slowly and emphatically.

"You see, I told you. Miss Prior won't let them."

"No! Miss Prior won't."

"Some people want our girls for brides as well. Varvara told me. You have seen the way old Mr. Bassgarden looks at us. But Miss Prior won't allow that either," said Mina.

Penny at last broke in. "No, Miss Prior certainly will not," she said.

The girls seemed at least somewhat reassured, so Penny continued.

"Matthew Cuthbert and the sorrel mare jogged comfortably over the eight miles to Bright River. When he reached Bright River there was no sign of any train; he thought he was too early, so he tied his horse and went into the station-house. The long platform was almost deserted, the only living creature in sight being a girl who was sitting on a pile of shingles at the far end. The station-master told him, 'There was a passenger dropped off for you. She's sitting out there on the shingles.' 'I'm not expecting a girl,' said Matthew blankly. 'It's a boy I've come for. He should be here.' The station-master replied, 'Guess there's some mistake. They gave the girl into my charge, and said that you and your sister were adopting her from an orphan asylum and that you should be along presently.'"

"Oh *noooo*, how awful! They sent the wrong child!" Katarine gasped.

"They will turn her out on the street. At least it's springtime and not winter."

"She was a child of about eleven, garbed in a very short, very tight, very ugly dress of yellowing gray wincey. She wore a faded brown sailor hat and extending down her back were two braids of thick and decidedly red hair. Her face was small, white and thin, and much freckled; her mouth was large and so were her eyes. In one hand she carried a shabby, old-fashioned carpet-bag. The other she held out to him."

"Red hair? Do people really have hair that is red?" asked Lusia.

"Silly, of course they do. Don't you know that Miss Webster the nurse has red hair?"

"I'd call that a brownish orange. Like a persimmon. Not red, like a pomegranate."

"Would you keep quiet and let Miss Prior read!"

"Matthew took the scrawny little hand awkwardly in his. He could not tell this child with the great wide eyes that there had been some mistake. And she could not be left at Bright River station anyhow, so all questions and explanations must be deferred until they were back at their farm, Green Gables. 'Oh it seems so wonderful that I'm going to live with you and belong to you! I've never belonged to anybody—not really. But the asylum was the worst. I've only been there four months, but that was enough. I don't suppose you were ever an orphan in an asylum, so you can't possibly understand what it is like. It's worse than anything you could imagine.'"

"Ha! That's where she is very, very wrong," said Yester.

"But when they arrived at Green Gables and Miss Cuthbert came out to meet them, she exclaimed, 'Matthew Cuthbert! Who is that? And where is the boy?' 'There wasn't any boy,' said her brother wretchedly, 'There was only *her*. I asked the station-master. I had to bring her home, as she couldn't be left there alone, no matter where the mistake had come in.' 'Well, this is a pretty piece of business!' said his sister.

"During this dialogue the child had remained silent, her eyes roving from one to the other, all the animation fading out of her face. Suddenly she seemed to grasp the full meaning of what had been said. Dropping her carpet-bag, she sprang forward a step, clasping her hands. 'You don't want me!' she cried. 'You don't want me because I'm not a boy!'

"'It's not like that,' said Miss Cuthbert. 'We need a boy to help Matthew on the farm. A girl would be of no use to us. We asked the orphan asylum to send us a boy.'

"'When the matron told me, you don't know how delighted I was. I couldn't sleep all last night for sheer happiness,' said poor Anne. 'You see, I've never had a real home since I can remember. My mother died of a fever when I was just three months old, and father died four days afterward from fever, too. I wish she had lived long enough for me to call her *mother*. So Mrs. Thomas took me in, but nobody wanted me, even then. I lived there until I was eight years old—I helped look after the Thomas children. There were four of them younger than me. Then Mrs. Hammond said she'd take me, seeing as how I was handy with children. She had eight, among them twins. I was *so* tired taking care of them all. I lived with them for two years, and then I had to go to the asylum. They didn't want me at the asylum, either, since they said it was already overcrowded. Nobody ever did want me. And now *you* don't want me because I'm not a boy!'"

"Oh, Anne!" cried little kind-hearted Katarine. "Ohhhh, Anne! It's so sad!" And she burst into tears.

"Now Katye, don't cry," said Nivart, embracing her. "You know the Cuthberts are going to change their mind. The book is called *Anne of Green Gables*, not *Anne of the Orphan Asylum*, nor *Anne of the Bright River Train Station*."

"So, Anne is a real true orphan. She never even knew her parents."

"Mrs. Thomas must have taken care of her . . . Anne was just a baby when she went to their house. So Mrs. Thomas was a sort of a mother."

"Only till Anne was old enough to work for her. Then she was a servant of the family. And after that, Mrs. Thomas gave her away."

"She gave her away. She *sent her away!*"

"Katye, it's only a story. Anne was not a real girl." This only made Katarine cry even harder.

Penny decided that, because of the direction she knew the story would be taking, she should not leave off at this point, but continue on as quickly as possible.

She did read on through Anne's adventures, the softening of Miss Cuthbert's heart, Anne's life at Green Gables, her school days and fun with her friend Diana, and her idyllic imaginings of all sorts. The novel followed her as she grew up, through her years at Queen's College, the death of loyal Matthew, Anne's return to care for his aging sister, and her budding romance with Gilbert Blythe. Most of the girls seemed charmed by Anne and her whimsical, volatile nature. But not Maritza.

Maritza was clearly provoked by Anne's emotional overreactions. "'I don't feel that I could endure the disappointment if anything prevented me from getting to the picnic!'" Maritza mocked. "That girl considers herself the queen of tragedy, over nothing. Because her dress doesn't have puffed sleeves. *Puffed sleeves,*" she repeated with contempt.

"You've got a point, Maritza," agreed Rosa. "She never stops flying into rapture or despair. I mean, suppose she had to face real tragedy, like war and starvation?"

"But she is a very romantic person," said Altoun. "She loves things very much."

"And not every child has lived through the things we have," Perouz noted quietly.

A few days after this, Maritza came to the hand-sewing room and spoke aside to Penny. "Today, Miss Prior, may I read something to the class? I have something, here." From a pocket she drew out a small, folded packet of paper. She had written something carefully on the back of her classroom worksheets—which she was not strictly permitted to do, since the classroom papers were kept and used again and again—but Penny was too intrigued by this to make an issue of the infraction.

Maritza sat down near Penny and began to read.

"The Story of Khoren and Araxie," she began. "By Maritza Markarian."

Once in an unlucky country there lived a girl named Araxie, in the village of Pinar, a town built on the sides of a steep ravine over a narrow, rushing river. Araxie had no brothers or sisters, but there was boy in the next house of her own age, and his name was Khoren. He too had no brothers or sisters. So they became playmates and the best of friends.

One day when Khoren drove his father's sheep back to the village after grazing them all day in the meadows, he found his house empty, the door flung open, the furnishings torn apart, as if some terrible struggle had taken place. Where were his father and his mother? The boy's heart shook with fear. As he stood there looking, Araxie flew out from the house next door, sobbing and beating her head with her fists.

She told him what had happened. A great war far away had suddenly come to their village, and their fathers and mothers, together with all of the Armenian men and women of the town, had been seized by the Turkish soldiers and marched away into exile in the desert. In all of Pinar there remained only very old people and a few children. Khoren was stricken with a storm of grief, fearing that he would never see his mother and father again.

'Just wait, dear Khoren,' Araxie said. 'It's too dark now, but in the morning we shall go after them, moving quickly and quietly, and we shall catch up to them. And I will be your sister and take care of you until we meet them again.' So they packed a small bundle with the bit of food that remained in their houses, and they slept on the floor huddled under the same quilt.

But that night the Kurds from the next steep valley came to their town, entered the houses, stole anything that was left, and carried off the remaining boys and girls as their slaves. Araxie and her 'brother' Khoren were taken by a big, burly, black-bearded man like an ogre, to his house in the Kurdish village. There Araxie was made to grind the grain in a stone mill and carry water from the fountain, and sweep the house and wash the clothes, while Khoren tended their captor's flocks.

They were not allowed to speak their own language, nor to pray to the Christian God. And they were kept apart from each other and beaten if they tried to be together. With great sorrow they realized that all hope of following their parents and finding them again had disappeared forever.

After many months of hard service, Araxie had a notion how they might escape. The two children were told to bring out the carpets from the house and clean them, so they were together again at last. Araxie whispered to Khoren in Armenian, 'Don't go to sleep tonight. When the moon stands over that tall pine-tree on the top of the hill, come silently outside, where I shall be waiting for you.'

Khoren's sleeping spot was on the floor at one end of the house, while Araxie slept upstairs near the Kurd's two wives. Both children contrived to pretend to be asleep, until they saw the moon climbing over the hilltop. Then Araxie crept out of the window and down a great old grape-vine to the ground, while Khoren slipped out of the door very quietly. Araxie had wrapped in a towel a tiny bit of bread and cheese and raisins that she had carefully saved from her own meager meals. And so the children slipped away.

They wandered for many weeks, searching for Armenian villages where a few people were left, begging for a little bread, and asking if the exiles from Pinar had passed by that way. Sometimes they were told, 'Yes, but many of them had already been killed, and the others were dying from hunger and the hardship of the journey.' And in fact, their parents' fate was never known, and nothing has been heard of them to this day. And the two of them were then the only family they ever had.

And when Araxie had led her 'brother' Khoren as far as she could, and they were weary unto death and had no food left, and their feet were bruised and bleeding, they came to a spring at the edge of a town called Reshaia. And at this spring they met a girl of their own age, drawing water from the fountain. She told them that she lived nearby, in an orphanage made by the Near East Relief to shelter Armenian girls. 'We must go there!' said Araxie. 'But will they take in boys, too?'

'Yes they will,' the girl replied. 'The boys' orphanage is in another town, some miles away.'

'But we must not be parted!' said Araxie, her eyes filling with tears.

'That's all right,' said the girl. 'Because you are brother and sister, they will allow you to stay together.' The girl assumed they were related because of the way they cared for each other.

The two children followed the girl to the orphanage and told the people there that they were brother and sister. And so it happened that they lived together at the orphanage, with a hundred and fifty girls and one boy, and Khoren was the pet of all the girls, but especially of his 'sister' Araxie.

But then it came to pass that Araxie fell ill with the summer sickness, and she tossed and turned upon her bed in a fearful sweat, aching in every limb. And her conscience plagued her because of the untruth she had told when first they came to the orphanage. And when the kind lady of the Near East Relief came to visit her in the

hospital, she confessed her lie, and admitted that they were neigh-
bors and friends but not brother and sister. And she wept bitter tears.
    'Someone is here to see you,' said the kind lady, and in came her
'brother' Khoren. 'No, we shall not send either of you away. For you
are as much of a sister to him as you could be, Araxie, and I am truly
proud of you.'

When Maritza had finished reading, there was a long silence, and then Maritza quickly stood up and left the room. The girls remained silent until the end of the sewing class, and then they filed out, leaving only Rosa behind.

"Miss Prior," Rosa began, "There is something I think you should know. Maritza did have a brother. A little brother, younger by a few years. And their village was emptied in the deportations, and their parents were taken away. They walked for a long time, looking for a safe place . . . but her little brother died along the way. She could not save him. And she is all alone now, the last of her family and her village."

"Thank you, Rosa," whispered Penny. She waited until the girl had gone, and then she wept.

The long barren winter continued. The world around them was firmly frozen, and a sense of emptiness pervaded their lives, inside and out. They all carried on with their necessary work, trying to make the best of what they had. But the land produced nothing at this time of the year, and the Near East Relief staff watched with anxiety as the supplies in their warehouses steadily dwindled. They were expecting new shipments—they lived in expectation of new shipments—but time passed and nothing came to them.

Penny continued to read to her girls in the sewing class. This mental respite from their threadbare existence was more valuable to them than ever. Penny gave Maritza a blank copybook of her own and two pencils, encouraging her to continue to write. But Maritza never mentioned the story she had shared; nor did she create new ones, except perhaps in secret.

Penny returned to her former room at the headquarters building, where she stored her steamer trunk, to fetch another book. The room was still shared by Doctor Eberlee and the nurse, Miss Webster. Opening the door, Penny was surprised to find Jane Eberlee lying on her army cot, fully dressed, eyes closed. Jane gave a start when Penny entered as if she felt guilty at being found there.

"Jane, are you all right?" Penny asked. "I'm sorry to disturb you."

"No, no, never mind. I was just . . . resting my eyes for a moment." Penny noted how pale Dr. Eberlee looked, and the shadowy rings around her eyes.

"You do seem very tired. Are you ill?"

"Not at all, just working too hard, I guess. Needed a bit of a break. I'll be fine." Jane got up and hustled around with a false show of energy and fitness. "Time I was getting back. See you at dinner, Penny."

At dinner, Penny sat with Arnaud and murmured very quietly to him, "Do you think Jane is all right? She seems a bit drained."

"Well, of course she's drained. I mean, why wouldn't she be? Our census is way up, all of these feeble freezing children scraped up off the streets, barely enough to feed them with. She and Dr. Artine both are working all the time. It helps a little that the trachoma hospital at Seversky Post has opened at last, and now it's Dr. Ruhl who looks after all of the eye-disease cases over there. But there is still plenty of infirmity here to keep our medics busy."

"I'm a little worried about her."

"Oh, now, you know better than that. Tough as a woodpecker is our Jane. She'll see it through, I've no doubt." But Arnaud's face told her that he did indeed harbor some doubt and concern.

Mr. Yarrow was making another of his inspection visits and had spent the whole day in the warehouses with Mr. Costen and Mr. Shears. He announced that he needed to speak with the whole staff over dinner.

"Friends and colleagues, I know that you receive very little news out here, and I have brought you some. But I'm sorry to say that not much of it is good news." Ernest Yarrow's long face and broad, thin-lipped mouth never did look very cheerful, but he was even more grim than usual that evening.

"You know that the Paris peace conference is getting nowhere. Over a year now with no progress. Nevertheless, the British are pulling out of key peace-keeping positions in Turkey, and the French are supposed to be occupying Cilicia and the Euphrates. But the French are not committing enough resources to do the job well. Granted, they are exhausted and have post-war problems of their own to deal with, but so do we all.

"At the same time, the Nationalist movement in Turkey, led by Mustafa Kemal, is gaining strength by the day. The presence of foreign troops in central and eastern Anatolia has enraged them. They have begun a campaign to expel all Europeans from Turkey, and with them the remnants of the Christian minorities that the Ottomans did not thoroughly destroy. Right now they have besieged the French in the city of Marash and the whole population is caught in the crossfire."

"Marash!" said Brownlea, the engineer. He had served there for several years as a missionary before the war.

"Yes, I'm afraid so. We are quite worried about the Near East Relief staff there, including the Wilsons and Stanley Kerr. And a member of the American Women's Hospitals, Dr. Mabel Elliott."

Jane Eberlee gasped and her hand flew to her mouth.

"So far as we know they are still all right, and we are monitoring the situation closely from Aintab. But if the Nationalists succeed there—and we expect that they will—we may see the movement carry on throughout eastern Turkey and right to the Armenian frontier."

"Oh no, not again," said Rufus Kendrick.

"And that's not all. They are also moving across the Black Sea coast, through Marsovan and Trebizond, and now, Batoum."

"The Turks are in Batoum?" said Arnaud.

"Yes, and that is why I must bring you the most unwelcome news of all. Batoum, of course, is the port through which almost all of the N.E.R. supplies reach the Caucasus. Without Batoum, we cannot resupply our stations."

"Oh Lord, no."

"However . . . the Turkish presence on the Black Sea is thin. We believe they have overextended themselves and cannot hold the territory as far east as Batoum. I have just now come from Erevan, where General Silikyan assures me that they can recover the port facilities soon. I have told him that it is absolutely essential that we bring in seed grain for the spring planting no later than the first of April. And really, we need food shipments long before that."

"Long before that," echoed Mr. Costen.

"Now, then," Mr. Yarrow continued, "I have asked every station in the Caucasus to go on half rations until further notice." A rumble of dismay rose from the room. "I know it will be difficult. I know that. But we must stretch our remaining supplies as far as we can, until the sea shipments can be reestablished. We are bringing in some supplies by rail through the Persian border and Baku, but the Caspian routes are expensive and unreliable. We must . . . tighten our belts for a while, that's all."

"These little children have no belts to tighten," said Jane, her voice tense.

"I know that, and I also know that we can trust all of you to put the welfare of the children first, even if it means going hungry ourselves."

Their empty winter became even emptier. Except for the very youngest and the children in the hospital, all of them gave up their canned condensed milk, an important component of their diet and the source of nearly all of their calcium, sugars, fats, and protein. They baked bread only every other day. Even their solid standby, corn grits, was rationed down to a tiny amount. Hunger was a daily reality for them all.

As it happened, Penny had started reading her class Frances Hodgson Burnett's book *A Little Princess*. It was the very melodramatic tale of the little daughter of a wealthy British officer in India who had sent her to be properly educated at a young ladies' boarding school in London, after the death of her mother. The child lived in luxury, as the star pupil of the haughty and avaricious Miss Minchin, headmistress of the young ladies' academy. The child's comfortable rooms and beautiful clothes and toys were described in lush detail.

Then came the news that the girl's father had died suddenly in India, upon losing his fortune through an unwise investment in diamond mines. The girl, Sara Crewe, was thrust at once into poverty. Miss Minchin took away all of Sara's fine belongings and turned her into a sub-tutor and errand maid at the school, sending her to live in a cold and sparse garret room at the top of the building.

"Why is it so bad to stay in a garret?" asked Veronika. "She has her own room. She's not living on the street."

"Compared to the fine lodgings she had before," explained Nivart. "With carpets of fur and her personal maid, and a wardrobe full of fancy clothes."

"Anne of Green Gables lived in a garret too. A garret is a place where orphans live, I guess."

"In books they do," said Badaskan.

Sara was badly treated by the vindictive Miss Minchin and the other school staff, deprived of meals, and sent out on errands in any weather. Her outgrown clothes became tattered and offered no warmth. "Sara now looked pale and thin, and at times she was almost ravenous with hunger. Her constant walking and running about on errands would have given her a keen appetite even if she had regular meals of a much more nourishing nature than the scraps that suited the convenience of the kitchen. 'You are so thin, Sara,' said one of the pupils. 'Look at the sharp little bones sticking out of your elbow!' 'I am *hungry*,' Sara said in a passionate voice. 'I am so hungry right now that I could almost eat *you*.'"

"Oh dear, are they going to be eating people again?" cried Katarine.

"The winter was a horrid one. There were days on which Sara tramped through snow on her errands; there were worse days when the snow melted and combined itself with mud to form slush, and the clouds hung low like mud, dropping heavy rain. The streets were chilly and sloppy and full of a dreary cold mist, drizzle and fog."

"London wasn't a very nice city."

"Not if you were poor, it wasn't."

"Sara was sent out again and again, until her shabby clothes were damp through. She was so cold and hungry and tired that at times a passer-by glanced at her with brief sympathy. But she persevered, as the muddy water squelched through her broken shoes and the wind tried to drag her thin jacket from her. She picked her way through the filthy streets as carefully as she could, and then she saw something shining in the gutter. It was a four-penny piece, trodden upon by many feet. And as she glanced up, directly before her eyes was a baker's shop, and a stout woman with rosy cheeks was putting into the window a tray of hot buns, fresh from the oven.

"But as Sara rushed to enter the shop, she saw something that made her pause. It was a little figure even more forlorn than herself, not much more than a bundle of rags, from which small, bare, muddy feet peeped out, and above the rags appeared a head of tangled hair, and a dirty face with big, hollow, hungry eyes."

"*Now* we are upon it," said Perouz. "*That* is what it means to be a homeless orphan."

"No garret, no nothing," added Veronika.

"Sara went into the shop. The woman looked at her intense little face and old bedraggled clothes. 'May I please buy four of those hot buns? The ones at a penny each?' The woman went to the window and put six of the buns into a paper bag. 'I'll throw in two for makeweight,' she said kindly. Sara could only thank the woman and go back out.

"The beggar girl was still huddled in the corner of the step, in her wet and dirty rags, staring straight before her with a stupid expression of suffering. Sara opened the paper bag and took out one of the hot buns. 'See, this is nice and hot. Eat it, and you will not feel so hungry.' The child snatched up the bun and crammed it into her mouth with great wolfish bites. Sara took out three more buns and put them down before her. Her hand trembled, but then she put down the fifth. Sara then walked on, and found some comfort in the remaining bun. She broke off small pieces and ate them slowly to make them last longer."

"That never really works," said Mina. "Just put it in your stomach and hope for the best."

And they all did that, in the ensuing weeks. Their half-rations kept them alive, but only just. On the days when bread was baked, Penny found herself secretly hiding her portion in a pocket. Later, she would give it unseen to a girl who looked especially frail and hungry. Soon, Penny had to sew tucks in the waistband of her skirt just to keep it from slipping off.

And on the first of March, Mr. Costen told them that there was one day's ration of wheat flour left, and two or three days of corn grits. The canned goods were finished except for the milk in the hospital stores, and he was not sure what they would do at the end of that week.

Jane and Penny went very early in the morning, before school started, to inventory the hospital stores themselves. Jane was dragging herself around so wearily that Penny insisted on helping her with basic chores at the intake hospital, where Penny still slept on her army cot.

When they reached the storeroom, they were alarmed to find the padlock open and the door ajar. A strange scene awaited them inside.

Ruben, the warehouse assistant to whom Bassgarden had delegated almost all of his few responsibilities, was lying on the floor surrounded by condensed milk cans that had been punctured with a screwdriver. Five of the cans were empty. A sixth had been opened and was in Ruben's fallen hand. When they understood what had happened, Penny lost the very last of her patience.

"You thief! You wretched criminal! How could you *do* this?" she screamed. "You stole enough milk to feed forty babies. Forty! You greedy pig!" In her fury she was actually kicking the soles of his feet, first one foot, then the other.

Jane Eberlee was kneeling over Ruben, feeling his pulse, opening his eyelids, touching his distended belly. "I suppose," she said quietly, "that he just couldn't stop himself wanting to feel his stomach really full, for once."

"How can you make excuses for him? He stole food right out of the mouths of helpless babies! I'm going to call the guards right now and have them throw him in the brig!"

"There wouldn't be much point in doing that, though, would there? Seeing as how he's already dead."

Penny froze in her frothing rage. She stared at the man's body again. Before her opened a yawning abyss of shame. She dropped right into it.

"Probably hyperglycemic shock . . . too much glucose in the bloodstream, too quickly," Jane continued. "Also dehydration. This product was never meant to be consumed without diluting it with water. He's been dead for hours. Kidney failure, then cardiac arrest, in my opinion."

Penny went to class after this, as duty required. But there was no reading that day. The girls observed her haunted, vacant face and said nothing.

And later that day came the first supply train chugging down the spur track and into the end-station at Kazachi Post. The blockade of the Batoum port had been broken.

CHAPTER 8

B ASSGARDEN was immediately relieved of his warehouse keys and banished from inventory control, just as supplies began flooding into their storage buildings with the revival of shipping through Batoum. He was assigned to oversee the new livestock program, since he claimed to be a "dab hand at administration," for the shipments now included large numbers of sheep and goats, dairy and beef cattle, piglets, chickens, ducks, and geese. Bassgarden knew nothing whatsoever about livestock, but the Armenian workers responsible for this department did, so it was felt that he could do little harm there.

He argued that he was the innocent victim of theft—that Ruben had stolen Bassgarden's keys and helped himself to the hospital stores—and they could not prove it false. So some gentle staffers favored a course of forgiveness. Arnaud, on the other hand, wanted to throw him out at once. The group decided to let him stay until Mr. Yarrow got a chance to decide what to do with him. Bassgarden had contrived to direct some money from the Lord Mayor's Fund to the orphanage projects in Armenia, so he had a tiny bit of leverage.

But just to keep things in order, Arnaud took Bassgarden aside and explained to him, in that relentlessly civil but savage manner that the English wield when they wish to, that if he put a foot wrong in any way Arnaud would make him regret it.

The arrival of ample and reliable shipments changed everything, especially because they were soon accompanied by a storm of new staff members that more than doubled their numbers. Suddenly there were 95 N.E.R. staff in Armenia instead of 45. Among these were new agriculture specialists, led by Professor Leonard Hartill, former head of the Department of Horticulture at the New York Institute of Applied Sciences. They were to organize the development of thousands of acres of land adjacent to the Posts, using new shipments of seed grain, teams of oxen, forty mules, and eleven Ford tractors, the first ever seen in the Caucasus.

Staff at the Posts increased from 22 to 30, including a new general practitioner, Dr. Eliza Mills, and two new nurses. Jane Eberlee was compelled to take a week off and rest, while Dr. Artine oriented the new physician.

Penny went to see Jane when she had a moment to spare, and found her writing letters home. The shipments had brought them their first mail delivery since last November.

"I thought I might find you here, doing this very thing," said Penny, smiling. "So I have brought two hot mugs of Hershey's cocoa, with Eagle Brand condensed milk and Horlick's malt. Isn't it wonderful to have these things again? I'm even delighted to open those cans of odious chipped beef stew."

"Wait till our new vegetable garden begins to produce. Imagine, fresh food . . . better than any medicine, especially for the little ones."

"My girls are bouncing around the sewing rooms with so much energy I can barely control it. A good thing too, since we've got mountains of used clothing bundles to go through. I think we can clothe the eight thousand orphans at the Posts and probably half of Armenia as well."

"Have you met the new Scoutmaster yet? My mother writes that the Boy Scouts are leading bundle drives all over the U.S. to collect clothing donations for the Near East Relief."

"Mr. Mason, yes—met him briefly, on his way to Polygon," Penny answered. "Took a moment to express our appreciation. He's got a very ambitious plan to organize Polygon into a sort of self-governing state led by the new Scout troop. I heard all about how he's going to indoctrinate them with the dignity of labor, personal morals and hygiene . . . what else did he say? Oh, practical religion and the upbuilding of character, the ideals of service and leadership. I wonder what they are going to make of him over there."

"They'll ask you to sew Scout uniforms next."

"Actually, the tailoring workshop at Polygon has already started doing just that. So I'm told."

They had not yet seen the high plateaus of Armenia in the spring. Suddenly the wide plains were suffused with the most delicate green, and patches of unexpected violets and buttercups appeared, then brilliant scarlet poppies. The watercourses roared with snowmelt, tinted a milky turquoise by rock sediment churned up in the rapid currents. They had to allow drinking water to settle before using it so that the particles could fall to the bottom. But the astonishingly fresh taste of the water seemed to imbue them all with extra energy.

Arnaud managed to arrange a couple of weeks in Tiflis with Orbeliani. The restaurants were offering greatly improved fare, though one could not inquire too closely about how these provisions reached them. Skimming of supplies to sell on the black market was commonplace behavior. Arnaud finally got the roast chicken he had been dreaming of.

The entertainment scene in the theatres, clubs, and concert halls of Tiflis had revived as well, including a strong underground cabaret culture. They were out late every night, then slept in all morning, then enjoyed their tea in the spring sunshine at a nearby cafe. It was not quite Paris or Berlin, but for them it was almost a vacation in Europe.

Because of Arnaud's visit to Tiflis, he was not present at Kazachi Post when the next goods train arrived carrying a passenger. An American, a Mr. Raymond Bundy. No one had invited him. No one was expecting him. And no one knew quite what to do with him. But because there was a firm and binding tradition of hospitality in that part of the world, they felt obliged to provide for him.

The housing manager reasoned that since they were both, in a way, guests of the Near East Relief and not staff, Bundy and Bassgarden could be accommodated together. So they were assigned to a men's housing annex above the restored carriage barn, now used for the Ford tractors.

The two of them immediately hit it off. They wandered all over Kazachi Post and Polygon (though they stayed away from Seversky Post and its contagious diseases), examining the work of others, asking many prying questions. They never missed a meal. And they spent many happy hours smoking together and discussing the state of the world.

"These Near East Reliefers," said Bundy. "They're really just a bunch of naïve Wilsonian idealists, aren't they?"

"Ye gods, yes," Bassgarden replied. "They think Woodrow Wilson is a humanitarian hero. All of this missionary-minded philanthropy of theirs. You know half of them served in Turkey or Persia with the American Mission Board. No sense of the realities of modern life. All of them want the United States to take on a political and military mandate to defend Armenia—a country that hasn't even any defined borders. What folly! And not in the proper way, as a colonial possession, but as a free and independent country."

"That's crazy. Armenia is the world's poorhouse. If you're going to take control of some faraway backwater, at least make it one that's rich in resources, am I right? You Brits always know how to do that," Bundy observed.

"It's no India, that's clear enough."

"Nothing to worry about there, though, since Congress voted against joining the League of Nations. The mandate's never going to pass."

"Did they indeed? I hadn't heard."

"Oh sure, in late March. The nineteenth, or thereabouts. You folks don't get much news out here, I reckon," Bundy added.

"Indeed. It seems that the United States will talk a grand game of serving the world, but they are not ready to take on the true burdens and responsibilities of global leadership."

"Hell, no. Just wait, our man Warren G. Harding will put a stop to all that. 'America First,' that's his motto. Harding and Hoover, they're not chumps like Wilson."

"Wilson's not the man he once was, in any event. Still filled with altruism, but quite out of touch. It's the end for his romantic internationalism, suffused with a religious mission. The world has moved on. The man meant well, of course, but he is a relic of the nineties," sniffed Bassgarden. "Not to mention a Presbyterian."

"What do you think are the chances for Armenia, then? If Congress rejects the mandate?"

"Probably quite dismal. Versailles produced no lasting consequences for Turkey, giving the Nationalists plenty of time to rearm and revive. Any post-war opportunity to free the world of Turkish bloody-mindedness has come and gone. You know they are overrunning central Anatolia right now, driving out the ineffectual French. And the Bolsheviks seem to be winning their civil war in Russia. Here is tiny helpless Armenia, trapped between those two foes."

"Doesn't look good."

"And what allies have they now? A lot of doctors, and agriculture professors, and orphanage managers, and Sunday School classes, and Boy Scouts? The N.E.R. is trying to carry out some of the functions of a mandate but with no political or military power. It's absurd. All they've got is weepy appeals for charity and a lot of sentimental posters."

"Those posters—oh, brother. A goddess wrapped in the American flag hugging a hungry little Armenian kid. I guess a lot of hayseeds out in the heartland are going to fall for that."

"If they only knew what Armenians are really like," Bassgarden said coldly. "You may have already discovered their unpleasantly combative nature. No proper deference to their betters. Unreliable, acquisitive, quarrelsome, self-seeking . . . prone to intrigue, and arrogance, and deceit. In point of fact, they're very much like the Jews."

"There's got to be a reason why they're always getting themselves persecuted."

"These everlasting appeals for aid . . . it's all getting to be such a bore. Nearly five years now we've been collecting for the starving Armenians. And every year, a new massacre or whatnot. The war is over. Yet these tiresome people and their professional uplifters are still wringing money out of the public."

"But you know, that's what editors like," replied Bundy. "The sob stuff. Tugging the heart-strings. Even better if there's something a little racy involved, like white slavery, women and girls held captive by the barbarous Turk, that type of thing."

"Old hat now, though, isn't it?"

"It does get harder to come up with a new angle. Now they want success stories, like such-and-such a little orphan who was saved by our generous help and is now healthy and happy and building the new Armenia."

"We have plenty of that going on here," observed Bassgarden dryly.

"Oh yeah, more than enough," Bundy muttered.

On one occasion their meddling activity brought them to the print shop, where Gordon Prior was teaching two young monks to set up the bookpress.

Bassgarden professed great pleasure at seeing the monks, asking for news of the Catholikos and life at Echmiadzin. This warmth might have seemed a little odd coming from someone who was willing to dismiss the entire Armenian people as deceitful, arrogant, and quarrelsome.

Gordon was only too happy to acquaint Bundy and Bassgarden with the inspiring nature of his mission.

"Here we are, with thousands of young children to educate," he was saying. "But education here is more than a pragmatic business. It's central to the restoration of the national character of these survivors, reconstructing them as a people. Reestablishing their language, culture, and history.

Do you know that many of the youngsters who come to us have forgotten how to speak their own mother tongue? We mean to help them recapture their heritage."

"Aren't you just raising a generation of little foreign Americans?" Bundy said.

"Oh no, not at all! These random waifs of the wayside are being given the tools to remake their own race. Yes, they shall benefit by learning American methods of productivity and efficiency, and leadership. We aim to replace the professionals and skilled artisans who were wiped out in the deportations . . . the pastors and scholars, the commercial class, the pillars of the community. These rescued orphans will become the leaders of the future. Leaven in the dough, causing the whole to rise."

"I say, Reverend Prior . . . isn't that a thoroughly elitist vision? You know as well as we do that the N.E.R. can absorb only a fraction of the needy children in this country. For every child in your orphanage, there may be ten more on the street, and another ten in families that can barely feed them. It's merely a drop in the proverbial bucket."

Prior gave Bassgarden a rather hard stare. "Nevertheless, our selfless service justifies our mission here. Ours is a stewardship for the welfare of the world. If even one per cent of the children of this nation adopt our example, it shall be a worthy sacrifice. Disinterested motives, that's the key. We come not to *be* leaders, but to *make* leaders. For the Armenian people."

Bundy and Bassgarden glanced at each other skeptically. "Sounds to me like you *do* want them to grow up to be just like you. Even though you said you didn't," Bundy remarked.

Prior felt himself ensnared, and it made him angry. "The Anglo-Saxon is tempted to believe that he alone is destined for a life of freedom and self-government, while others are never fit for it. Democratic at home, imperialist abroad. But our mission schools have always been engines of innovation and enlightenment. These books . . ." Prior said, picking up some of the products of the print shop. "They will equip the children here for critical thinking and independence. For full and free citizenship. And then, when they are grown, they can make of Armenia whatever they wish."

"Not if the Bolshies get here first," said Bundy.

"Will you excuse me? I'm rather busy this afternoon."

People tried not to sit near Bundy and Bassgarden at meals, but they could not always be avoided.

"So . . . Doctor," said Bundy as a challenge to Jane Eberlee at dinner. "You ever wonder why we're feeding so much corn to the Armenians? They've never grown corn in this part of the world before."

Jane, believing that this was a serious question, answered, "Ground corn is a healthy whole grain, easily digested and calorie-dense. It's filling, simple to transport and store. Certainly useful for patients who haven't eaten in a long time . . . their ability to digest starches is much reduced by starvation. As long as re-feeding is gentle and gradual. Even very young children can eat it."

Penny, sitting beside her, joined in. "And you don't even need an oven to bake it in. Just water and some heat. You can cook it over a fire in a tin can."

Bundy chuckled. "Oh ladies, I can see that you have a lot to learn. Look at all these grits. And this beef, fed by corn. And this condensed milk, sweetened with corn syrup. What you see here is a triumph of the American agricultural machine. Midwest farmers are unloading all of their surplus corn on you."

"Well, we are grateful for it, just the same."

"Don't you see? They are aiming to create new export markets in the Near East. Once people are accustomed to it, they'll be willing to buy it. Much cheaper than wheat. Corn's not very popular in the U.S. yet—the consumer market is paltry."

"At home, we feed corn only to animals," said Bassgarden haughtily.

"But here's the true genius of it," said Bundy. "By donating tons and tons of corn to the relief, the growers get terrific publicity. They can say that their product is so wholesome that doctors are using it to rescue starving people. What American mother doesn't want her children to grow up well-nourished? They'll start buying this miracle food for their own offspring, and then it's off to the races. They've even got N.E.R. people talking up Karo corn syrup. That's marketing, my friends."

"The American Relief Administration provides it to us."

"Sure they do. They have good reasons to shore up the American farming industry. And it's not just corn, it's all this canned milk. Dairy price supports, very popular in Congress. And right here, this Hershey's cocoa. Hershey donated twenty-five thousand pounds of chocolate to the Near East Relief. After the war they had all of this excess production capacity and no soldiers to feed. What to do with it? Send it to the starving Armenians! There's nothing like big-time charity to get yourself good press."

"If they are doing a good deed, they deserve good press," asserted Penny.

"You're thinking much too small. We've got the whole of the Western economy right here on our plates. Corporations, the government, and the nonprofit sector, all working together to make capitalism hum along like a top. Makes you proud to be an American."

Jane and Penny both looked at him, and Penny sighed. "Thank you for that information, Mr. Bundy," Jane said courteously, and they both got up and left.

Bundy watched them leave. "Stand-offish bunch, aren't they?" he said.

"You have no idea," Bassgarden replied.

Not long after this, Raymond Bundy departed, without ever giving them any explanation for his presence there. Poor Bassgarden was reduced to annoying everyone all by himself.

Good weather for construction made it possible for them to rehabilitate more of the old buildings at the Posts; they could hire many more laborers, paid with old clothing and corn grits. They could afford to take on new orphan carers and increase their boarding census, taking in more of the pleading youngsters who clustered around their gates and accosted them in towns.

They also began making plans to reach some of the outlying towns and villages, those not on the main rail lines. Especially in the mountains, there were urgent needs, including many orphaned children being cared for through a traditional system of informal fostering, but without resources or aid.

A journey was completed to establish a new relief center at the town of Jelal-Oghlu, in the forested Lori district, up in the mountains above Ghara Kilisa, about forty miles from the Posts at Alexandropol. The distance was shorter as the crow flies, but the mountainous terrain required careful climbing and tight switchbacks. Trucks were not able to reach it yet due to the state of the roads. Some of the roads were more like trails. Food and other necessities had to be packed in by mule convoys, and that process had already started.

Jelal-Oghlu was the regional hub from which many villages could be supplied, and it had the great asset of another imperial barracks compound, now transferred by the Erevan government to the Near East Relief. When fully restored, it could accommodate up to 2500 children. The valley in which the barracks stood could be cultivated to produce food, and the forest surrounding it would provide fuel, another scarce commodity further south.

The next supply trip was planned for mid-April. Dr. Artine was going up to assess the medical needs of the population, and Sahag Asdourian would investigate the schools there, hire teachers and arrange their training. He invited Gordon and Penny Prior to come as well and visit a part of the country they had not yet seen. Penny's friend Alma would go with them and remain at Jelal-Oghlu to manage that intake hospital, along with two of their experienced Armenian teachers.

The journey across the high plateau as far as Ghara Kilisa was level, on relatively decent roads, so they could cover most of the distance and stay there in safe accommodation overnight. One wagon was fitted with benches to make passengers a bit more comfortable, though they were still perched upon sacks of flour and corn grits. Armed guards led and followed them on horseback.

"We won't be far from the Georgian border up there," Mr. Asdourian explained. "The mountain tribes keep to their many languages and traditional ways of life . . . it's called 'The Mountain of Tongues' by some. Every steep gorge preserves its own tiny culture. I'm not even sure how much they want Armenian schools."

"I'm afraid that it soon won't be a matter of what they want," said Dr. Artine. "There is every kind of political ferment in the cities now. A little newspaper for every shade of opinion: Leninists, Trotskyites, Denikinists, Anti-Denikinists, Islamic radicals, anarchists, nationalists, Mensheviks, Dashnaktsutyun, Social Democrats, Green Guards, Socialist-Revolutionaries, Left-Socialist-Revolutionaries, and so on and so forth. Many of these parties are just a handful of former students in a shabby hotel room. All of them are trying to position themselves to become a part of whatever new order they believe is on its way."

"They are proclaiming their own governments already. The Black Sea Province Peasants' Republic. What is that? The Independent Mountain People's Government. The Central Caspian Dictatorship." Asdourian shook his head. "They are like mushrooms, springing up overnight. Ridiculous, really, but possibly quite dangerous too."

"Most of them are Bolsheviks in essence, are they not?" asked Gordon Prior. "And Bolsheviks are always atheists. They will move to suppress the Church and every expression of the Christian faith."

"Very likely," Asdourian said. "They believe the churches possess treasure that they can plunder. Also, they say that religion keeps the workers and peasants contented with their lot in life, unwilling to undertake the proletarian revolution. It may be a dark day if they make their way down to Erevan."

The second day of travel took them up and up, into the dramatic alpine environment of the Lori. Each deep gorge was more beautiful than the last, cloven by countless streams and turbulent, narrow, rocky rivers. Above them towered the rim of the mighty Caucasus range, laden with a permanent snowpack, flashing with a blinding light whenever the clouds parted to strike the peaks with a beam of sun.

They paused for a travel rest at an accessible stream where the mules could be watered. Penny was enchanted with the beauty of the forests . . . it reminded her how much she missed the woods near Oberlin where she would go alone and pour out her heart in prayer.

Following a streak of sunlight filtering down through the budding birch trees, she wandered away into the forest. Under her feet were carpets of minute white galanthus, dangling from their stalks like bells; in every fully shaded spot beneath thick pines were drifts of stubborn snow. There was a feeling of warmth, then chill, then warmth again, and a wonderful scent of incipient life. Her heart was swelling with joy. She closed her eyes and raised her hands, her lips moving soundlessly in thanks and praise.

Hearing the jingling snort of a horse or mule, she opened her eyes, and stopped short. Surrounding her was a loose squad of men on horseback, most of them armed, some of them in uniform. One of the men dismounted, stepped forward and wrenched her service revolver from the holster on her Sam Browne belt.

"Wait—I don't think you should do that," she said in her soft voice. "I believe that is the property of the United States government."

"What are you doing out here?" asked one of them, in Armenian. "Don't you know that these forests are full of wolves and bears?"

"Well, I'm . . . I'm travelling with the Near East Relief party. We're going up to supply the orphanage at Jelal-Oghlu."

"You may be a little late for that. These ruffians have taken over the barracks complex there. The Red Army is in Armenia now."

One of the men on horseback, in a brown uniform and a soft peaked cap with a red star, barked at him, presumably in Russian. He was a small man, with close-cropped dark hair and penetrating black eyes. But it was the other man—a thin fellow with a fair complexion and an apologetic manner—who spoke to her, again in Armenian.

"This is Comrade Garmakov—he thinks he's in charge here. My name is Grigor Chalakyan. I'm a teacher at Jelal-Oghlu, in the government school. At least I was, before I got captured by these brutes. Who are you?"

"My name is Penelope Prior. I'm an orphanage assistant with the Near East Relief. Does he know what that is? We shelter and clothe and feed little children. That's all."

Grigor translated this for Garmakov, but not very well. Instead of "feed little children," he mistakenly said that they "eat little children." All of the Russians looked at him with a shocked expression, and then unexpectedly burst out laughing.

There was a spirited exchange among them in Russian, which Penny could not understand. She had no idea what struck them as funny.

Garmakov looked at her more closely, then said something. "He wants to ask—how old are you?" said Grigor.

This question always irritated Penny. "I don't know how that could be any of your business," she replied.

"She says she doesn't know," translated Grigor.

Garmakov stared at her even more intently. "How could she not know how old she is?" he demanded, in Russian.

"What they are discovering is that I don't speak much Russian at all," said Grigor. "I never wanted to be their translator. I'm hoping to do such a poor job that they let me go and get someone else to do it."

"Well, see if you can tell him this. They are a lot of Bolsheviks and atheists and I reject that. Neither force nor flattery can change me. I am a true Christian and a woman of honor, and if they try to compel me to follow them, God will punish them for it."

Grigor told Garmakov something, though it was not clear how much of her statement got through. They gathered that she had no intention of cooperating with them. Garmakov replied in an offended tone.

"He says they are Red Army, not stinking politicals," reported Grigor. "They're not goons of Stalin or a pack of Mauserists."

"A pack of what? Maybe you didn't translate that right. I don't even know what a Mauserist is."

"You know what? Neither do they!" This time Grigor and Penny shared a snicker that the others could not comprehend.

At length, Comrade Garmakov decided to take Penny back to her travelling party, and a complex discussion ensued with Dr. Artine, who spoke excellent Russian. Garmakov explained that his company was only passing through Jelal-Oghlu and did not intend to occupy it. He said that he had nothing against sheltering and clothing and feeding little children, so long as they didn't eat any of them. The Russians all laughed again at this remark.

Garmakov returned Penny's service revolver, and the soldiers departed.

The Near East Relief group stayed for several days at the barracks compound in Jelal-Oghlu, carrying out their responsibilities there. It seemed to them that the local leadership was strong and needed mainly a steady flow of supplies from Alexandropol.

While they were still there, Grigor the unwilling interpreter was dismissed by Comrade Garmakov and found his way back to Jelal-Oghlu. Sahag Asdourian was able to work with him on ways that the Near East Relief could help the government school there.

They also discovered that the area was becoming well known as a hotbed of Armenian Communism, initiated by a fiery individual named Stepan Shahumyan, one of Lenin's infamous Baku Commissars, who had been executed by a firing squad early in the revolution. With the defeat of the White Russian "Volunteer Army," it seemed that their day had finally come.

And indeed, that day turned out to be the twenty-seventh of April 1920, when the Bolsheviks overthrew the government in Baku and declared a new Azerbaijani Soviet Republic. They seized control of the oil fields and arrested all British subjects, including the Consul and functionaries in the petroleum industry.

And in May came the news of a Bolshevik uprising in Tiflis, their Georgian neighbor to the north. Then, on the first of June, the United States Senate voted against accepting a mandate to defend Armenia. So there they were, floating alone on a tiny raft of Armenian independence in a vast ocean of revolution and reactionary dictatorship.

Forces of the Russian Red Army continued to flow into the country, comfortably moving south, meeting negligible resistance. An Armenian Bolshevik alternative government already existed, the Revolutionary Committee or Revkom. They were drinking tea in the mountains and waiting for their Russian comrades to hand over Erevan to them.

A powerful representative of the Russian Communist Party, Boris Legran, arrived in Erevan to dictate terms of surrender to the helpless Dashnak government. The Dashnaks sought only to negotiate immunity from reprisals for themselves, on the basis of their full submission to the new world order.

Legran presented a draft document spelling out these terms to the Cabinet late in the afternoon, and then to the final gathering of the Parliament that night. There was no electricity in the Parliament chamber again, so that meeting took place by candlelight. The darkness rather suited the occasion.

There was a little perfunctory debate, without hope, without energy, making some minor corrections and changes to be incorporated into the draft, creating a semblance of actual consent. And then they took a vote. The Parliament approved the compact with Soviet Russia and the formal transfer of power in Armenia, by a vote of 22 to 9.

The Revkom was summoned down from their mountain retreat near Lake Sevan. The Cabinet resigned. All government officials were ordered to remain at their posts and submit to the new regime. The military was transformed into the Red Army of Soviet Armenia and all ranks were abolished. The city of Erevan was quiet, despondent; members of the former government dispersed to their homes. All imprisoned Bolsheviks were released and treated to a celebratory reception in the Parliament building.

Someone took the initiative to confiscate the printing press in the Orthodox monastery at Echmiadzin, so they were able to publish the first issue of the *Komunist* newspaper, proclaiming the existence of the new Soviet Socialist Republic of Armenia.

In honor of this popular revolution of the workers and peasants, two cavalry brigades and a regiment of infantry marched down Abovian Boulevard to the city center. And a page was turned in the long, anguished, complex and often futile story of the Armenian people.

CHAPTER 9

"THE politicals are fanatics. Ruthless. They do not care if everyone starves for their ideals. Truly, they do not. To me, that is utterly foolish. Of what use to the revolution is a shattered Armenia? Why not a successful and productive one instead? Surely a workers' and peasants' state needs to have some living workers and peasants in it."

Comrade Garmakov was addressing the meeting he had called in his new offices at Alexandropol. As the appointed Commissar for the northern provinces, he was now responsible for the area comprising Kazachi Post, Seversky Post and Polygon, as well as outlying district locations such as Jelal-Oghlu.

He had summoned Mr. Yarrow from Erevan and several of the staff members from the Posts, asking specifically for Doctor Artine, Sahag Asdourian, and "the girl who doesn't know how old she is," meaning Penelope Prior. Her father protectively came along with her.

Their purpose was to work out an agreement between the Near East Relief and the new Soviet government in Armenia. Garmakov shrewdly reasoned that he might get ahead of the "politicals" in Erevan by establishing a regional agreement first, one that they could use as a model if they were so inclined.

Garmakov wanted to see orphans looked after and people employed, regular harvests on their way, and some stability restored to the country. He knew that the N.E.R. had the resource network to make these things happen and the new government did not.

"It must be clear to you," Ernest Yarrow said carefully, "That we are not political agents in any way. Ours is a purely humanitarian organization. The Near East Relief is not interested in ideology, but in service . . . saving lives, rebuilding Armenia's ability to support itself."

"They won't like that . . . if by 'rebuilding' you mean reproducing a Western capitalist system here in the Caucasus."

"There is nothing specifically 'capitalist' about our plans to develop this region's agriculture," said Leonard Hartill, the horticulture professor. "In fact, you could consider what we are doing around Alexandropol to be this country's first collective farming. The produce belongs to the population, not to a landlord."

"Leninakan," said Garmakov.

"Pardon me?"

"This city is now known as Leninakan. Don't you know that Alexandropol was named after the Tsar's wife, Alexandra? They mean to sweep away all of that. I can only say, 'Fine, you rename cities while we carry on here and do what needs to be done.' I must tell you, though, you do not understand collectivism as these people practice it. To them, all of the produce belongs not to the population, but to the state. They want to control all of the village grain, then require people to earn back their own confiscated property through public works projects, irrigation canals, roads, other labor. Do you see the difference?"

"We pay workers for their labor with grain."

"Ha! You pay them with *your* grain, not with their *own* grain! You are not ready to deal with these people. That is obvious."

"Can you help us?" asked Ernest Yarrow humbly.

"I believe so. I hope so. At least, until they conclude that I am really a counter-revolutionary and put me in front of a firing squad."

Their conversation was, in fact, much slower than this, since it was taking place simultaneously in English, Russian and Armenian, and remarks often had to be translated twice. They had brought Comrade Garmakov a gift of tea and sugar. A huge samovar was kept boiling all day, while they laboriously worked out specifics in a document that they hoped would protect all parties.

The Near East Relief pledged to pursue no political objective, motive or purpose, nor to represent or promote any particular form of political, social or industrial organization.

"That isn't strictly accurate," Gordon Prior objected. "We do employ American methods and advocate for American structures of work and life, in the form of our example."

"I don't doubt that," Garmakov replied. "And they will say that every act is a political act, anyway. They won't believe that you can pledge to be non-political."

"So why agree to that statement?"

"Because it gives them the power to judge you, and they will insist on that. There will be no agreement without something of the kind."

They also agreed to eschew all commercial or material objectives, pledging not to promote any private business or trade enterprise, nor to derive any benefit from such ties. They had to acknowledge that this was not strictly accurate, either.

"Most of our flour, ground corn and seed grain comes through a partnership between private American growers and the United States government," Mr. Yarrow explained. "We can't avoid it. At least, not until Armenia achieves its own cereal production."

"I'm not sure they will even grasp that," said Garmakov. "These are philosophers who want to decree communal prosperity but have little knowledge of farming, factories, railroads, or any kind of industry. They don't even really understand how government works. They think everything can be imposed from the top down and somehow it will happen."

"It seems to me," Penny ventured, "That Bolshevism and Tsarism are practically the same. You've just gone from one set of rulers to another."

Everyone in the room looked uncomfortable at this. Finally someone said, "Isn't that why they call it the dictatorship of the proletariat?"

The document committed the Near East Relief to continue their services to the needy, agreeing to relieve suffering in any form within its power. The new government undertook to protect their operations from interference, to recognize the consular rights and physical security of all foreign nationals on their staff, and to confirm their tenancy of all buildings and lands occupied by the N.E.R. Their relief stores, local products, machinery and equipment were to be exempt from requisition, taxation, rent, or customs duties. Ernest Yarrow gave an audible sigh of relief when these conditions were stipulated.

There were further clauses defining their access to railroads, telegraph, mail and other communications, and to utilities such as water and electricity, and their right to purchase fuel supplies. They were allowed to harvest lumber for fuel from the forests around Jelal-Oghlu.

"Stepanavan," the Commissar corrected them. "The town of Jelal-Oghlu has been renamed in honor of the Bolshevik martyr Stepan Shahumyan."

"Of course it has," someone commented dryly.

"There is one other issue that I hesitate to include in this document, because I don't want to call their attention to it," continued Garmakov. "You know that they are already moving against the Patriarch in Echmiadzin, confiscating church property, closing churches, curtailing religious instruction. This is a thing that they understand and care about."

"But of course we provide religious education at the Posts," said Gordon Prior. "We're not about to stop that. All of the children worship at the Kazachi Post church, Saint Arsenius. We employ two Armenian Apostolic clergy to perform the *badarak*—the Divine Liturgy. It's essential to the healthy development of our children."

"They will not agree. They will call it reactionary indoctrination of the young. I'm only warning you, it *will* stop."

A blanket of gloom settled upon them. Garmakov promised to try to protect their right to worship at the Kazachi Post church and to have clergy there, but he told them forthrightly to expect that religious instruction in the classroom was now over.

For someone with such disdain for "politicals," Garmakov proved to be a skilled political operator himself. He managed over the course of the next few months to get their agreement approved up the chain of command, signed by Askanaz Mravyan of the Revkom, General Secretary of the Communist Party and People's Commissar for Foreign Affairs of Soviet Armenia, and then by Charles Vickrey of the Executive Committee of the Near East Relief in New York. This achievement did not solve all of their problems by any means, but it proved a durable basis for coexistence.

With a strong supply chain and steadily advancing skills among their local people, the N.E.R. programs in the Caucasus blossomed. Eventually they took 36,000 acres of land under cultivation, using 22 American tractors. Boys and men were trained both as mechanics and tractor operators. Rufus Kendrick was happily teaching youngsters to replace himself.

By now, in addition to the cereal harvest, they were producing a good quantity of garden crops, such as beets, potatoes, carrots, onions, cucumbers, squash, cabbages, and many varieties of healthy greens. Their diet had improved enormously. They were raising dairy cows, beef cattle, sheep, hogs, and goats on 16,000 acres of pasture land, and whole flocks of ducks, geese, and egg-laying hens.

These creatures produced hides, wool, and feathers, raw materials for their industrial training. There was still very little cotton locally available, but importing it had become much easier.

Penny was able to design a multi-level intensive clothing program using the leadership of experienced girls to teach and guide the younger ones. The hand-sewing class had evolved into a dressmaking studio. With the Polygon orphanage and its increased tailoring and shoemaking capabilities, they were beginning to produce a surplus of items that could easily be sold or traded to provide for other needs.

But many more kinds of industrial training were now developing at both Posts, mostly along gendered lines. The girls learned domestic tasks, such as food preparation and storage, baking, cooking, and creamery, laundry and ironing, the making of mattresses and keeping them clean and repaired, wool-washing and carding, spinning, weaving and knitting, lace-making and crochet, embroidery, dyeing, even basketry and the making of straw hats, which quickly became very popular.

Gordon Prior's bookbinding group continued to excel, producing enough textbooks for both schools and beginning to supply those at other posts, too.

The boys at Polygon had a wider range of options available, including carpentry and construction, masonry and plumbing, iron, copper, brass and silver smithing, mechanical engineering of many kinds, the creating of brushes and brooms, window glazing, pottery and the production of crockery, including great vessels for fermenting and pickling vegetables for winter.

Using their large supply of empty milk cans, the boys turned out tin lanterns, stoves, dustpans, bowls and cups, clever toys. Even baling wire and packing crates were repurposed. The work involved in the farming operation also meant designing irrigation systems, establishing roads, building barns and sheds, fencing pastures.

Vocational training served as a substitute for the kind of learning that normally would happen in the home and family. A mother would teach domestic skills to her daughters, and boys would often follow in their father's footsteps, picking up his trade. But at the Posts, they were obliged to do their parenting on a massive scale.

The Near East Relief orphanages in the Caucasus eventually reared over 30,000 children. Nearly 18,000 lived and grew up at Polygon and Kazachi Post. A city of orphans. The largest childcare center in the world.

Penny Prior had little perspective on the larger whole. She was firmly focused on her girls in the sewing classes.

"Rosa, that's very good! *Shad aghvor!* The detail on the collar and the ribbon, I like it."

"But it's not exactly what I wanted. When I try it on, the collar doesn't lie flat."

"Oh, I see. I think we can fix that," Penny said, quickly pulling out the basting stitches and repinning it. "Here, try basting it like this, and see if that helps."

"Thank you, Miss Prior."

Penny became aware that Maritza Markarian was standing off to one side of the room, waiting for her. She made her way over in that direction.

"Excuse me, Miss Prior . . . I want to tell you that I have finished translating the first story in *The Red Fairy Book*. I think it is ready to read now."

"Oh, that's wonderful, Maritza! Did you find it difficult? Your English is so much stronger than it used to be."

"The story is easy to follow, you know . . . twelve dancing princesses, sneaking out of the palace at night . . . their father wants to know where they are going . . . there is a simple cowherd named Michael, who of course is an orphan, with a magic flower that makes him invisible. He follows them, learns their secret, and wins the youngest princess and becomes a prince. Altoun will like it, because the cowherd is curly-haired and handsome," added Maritza.

"No doubt," Penny agreed.

"I left out some of the bits that were just beside the point. But I did like the hidden groves of trees with leaves of silver, leaves of gold, and leaves of diamonds. You can expect that the story would have something like that, because that's how these stories go."

"True—they do tend to follow a pattern. I suppose that is one of the things people like about them, especially the children. If you find any unknown vocabulary, please don't hesitate to ask me, or Mr. Asdourian."

"He did help me. He is happy that I am doing this."

"I'm sure he is. It's always very gratifying when a student begins to mature and act on her own." Penny looked at her with genuine affection, and Maritza smiled shyly. "The reading club does need some more material. It's too bad they didn't really enjoy Dickens. Oliver Twist, David Copperfield, even Little Nell . . . they didn't care for those stories, for some reason."

"Perhaps, too many orphans. Too much sadness, and too many people being cruel. It hurts to be reminded all the time of what we have lost, of what we will never have. I think we need to put something very different into our minds. Images of trees with leaves of diamonds. Dragons, swans, knights in armor, beautiful places, magical things. It lifts the heart, even though the stories are so unreal."

"I see what you mean."

"I think we need to learn some Armenian folk tales, too. The girls here remember some . . . and I want to ask the ladies who work at Kazachi Post if they know any they can tell me. We might be able to write a book of stories for our children from their own people."

"Yes! Oh yes, that would be lovely! Why couldn't we print it right here, on our own bookpress? And perhaps Mr. Arnaud and his drawing class could make illustrations for it."

Maritza's eyes were shining. Penny had never seen her so engaged before. "I am thinking this, too. This very thing. Stories, songs, poems, prayers . . . everything that Armenian mothers would give their little children, in their own home." Her voice sank to a whisper. "For all of the children whose mothers are gone."

Penny took the girl's hand and pressed it, gently. "There is something else I meant to ask you about, Maritza . . . I want you to consider this. You are a skilled seamstress now, and an excellent teacher of the younger girls. At sixteen, our girls can leave us, and marry, and start their own families, if they wish."

"I don't want that," Maritza replied quickly.

"I understand, and that is fine, too. But my point is that you are old enough to be hired as a member of our orphanage staff. You could teach sewing classes, and also work on our literature project. You would earn a salary and you could live with the other teachers. We could be colleagues, now."

Maritza's eyes widened, and her face became very serious. "I need to think about this," she replied.

"Of course, take all the time you need. But please know that I believe you are ready."

"Thank you, Miss Prior."

"You should call me that in the classroom, and I shall call you Miss Markarian. But I want you to feel free to think of me as Penny, among ourselves."

Maritza seemed about to respond to this, but instead she quickly left the room.

Penny needed some time to herself that afternoon, once classes were over. She did not want to disturb Jane Eberlee and Miss Webster in their room, and the intake hospital afforded no privacy. So, she took her portfolio, pens, and ink over to the Saint Arsenius church.

She had befriended one of the elderly deacons of the church, a *sarkavag*, and he allowed her to sit in the library when the priests were not using it. It was a library almost bereft of books, after the ravages of war and pillaging. But there were some tables and chairs, so she could spread out her writing paper and answer her letters from home.

It was much more enjoyable to write home now that they could receive and send mail in a timely manner. Also, she wanted to tell her mother Wellandette and her sister Tildy more about her life, now that things were going better at Kazachi Post.

She had felt no desire to write and tell them about the bitter winter weather, or how hungry they all were, or how hopeless it all seemed when their shipments were delayed. These days, she could come up with details and incidents that pleased her and might perhaps please them, too.

After writing for over an hour, Penny prepared to leave. But first, she had to stop in the great sanctuary and pray.

It was quiet and dim in there as usual, with a little daylight entering through the very high windows, and some isolated flickers of candlelight. A sweet, smoky trace of incense hung in the air. Lifting her hands and closing her eyes, she slipped into her attitude of deep prayer. She had many things to feel thankful for.

When she had finished, she found the old deacon waiting for her by the door.

"Oh, forgive me, *sarkavag*," she said in Armenian. "Is it time to lock up? I'm sorry you had to wait for me."

"Never mind that," he said with a gentle smile. "You have the glow of the Holy Spirit. When God fills us, that is all that matters."

She looked at him with surprise. "The glow?"

"God is like the fire, filling the iron with heat. We are the iron, dark and cold, until the heat causes it to glow." He paused. "Some people say that God is like the light, shining into the world, and this is true. But the eyes are not enough, the mind is not enough. We *feel* God like we feel the heat. Do you understand?"

"I think so . . ."

"The philosophers, the thinkers—we need them. But the Spirit is not in our philosophical speculation, nor in our literary conceits. The Spirit is in the glow of the heart."

Penny stood quietly, absorbing this. Finally she said, "Thank you, *sarkavag.*"

"*Astvats orhni qez,*" he replied. "God bless you."

Penny had time to do one more thing before heading to the dining hall for their evening meal. She leafed quickly through the new magazines that had just arrived for her through the postal delivery. They had made an arrangement for her to receive a few popular magazines from the United States on a fairly regular basis, so she could see the drawings in advertisements of clothing for women and children, and use them in the dressmaking class. These were not high-fashion magazines, but ordinary periodicals intended for middle-class homes, with news and feature articles for the general reader.

Glancing through them, her eye caught the word *CAUCASUS*, and she stopped at once to look at it more closely.

PLAYING GOD IN THE CAUCASUS . . . that was the title. *The Near East Relief Holds the Power of Life and Death over Survivors of War and Deportation.* Sucking in her breath, she read a few paragraphs. She looked at the byline. *By Raymond F. Bundy.* Clutching the magazine, she hurried over to the dining hall.

"Jane! Arnaud! You need to see this!" she exclaimed as they seated themselves at the table. She read aloud to them and the others nearby. "*The doctor decides, like the Angel of Death, which of the sick and hungry children shall be saved. Will this be one of the lucky ones who gets a place in the N.E.R. orphanage? Or will she condemn him to a slow and painful death by starvation?*"

"Oh, dear Lord," breathed Jane Eberlee.

"*We have all seen the photographs of corpses strewn across the desert, of tottering living skeletons on city streets. These images are skillfully used in publicity campaigns to wring donations out of kind-hearted Americans. N.E.R. advertising has appeared in more than 3000 newspapers and 1500 trade publications. They are selling compassion like tooth powder, and the money is rolling in.*"

"Selling compassion?" Arnaud objected. "That doesn't even make sense. What kind of editor let that go by? Which cheap rag is that, anyway?"

"It's *The Investigator*. The May issue, which we just got today."

"How could he do that to us?" asked Doctor Eberlee. "We welcomed him. We showed him hospitality. He sat here at our table and then went away and wrote that?" Bassgarden was sitting at the far end of their table, and they all turned their heads to look at him. He studiously kept his eyes on his plate.

"There is much more," said Penny. "*And what kind of money is it? We all remember the 'Tainted Money' scandal of 1905, when the robber baron John D. Rockefeller donated $100,000 to the American Board of Commissioners for Foreign Missions. Having derived those profits from deliberately destroying his competitors in the rail freight industry, he then sought to 'launder' those ill-gotten gains through philanthropy. And many Americans were either tempted or fooled. Captains of commerce today are making large donations to the Near East Relief. But is it possible to do the Lord's work with the Devil's dollars?*"

"Ohhhhh . . . of all the bloody tripe," growled Arnaud. "That worthless git."

"If people read that stuff, will they still want to donate to the Near East Relief?" Rufus Kendrick asked. "Perhaps they will stop giving. If they do that, it's our children who will suffer. Doesn't he care about them?"

"*Farmers donate their corn and wheat surplus with the aim of creating new export markets in the Near East. Working closely with the Corn Products Refining Company and the Midwest Grain Growers Board, they try to convince Americans that these products are also healthy for their own families, to increase domestic consumption. And, since the Revenue Acts of 1913 and 1917, these corporations can gain charitable tax deductions by sending their cocoa, milk, macaroni, and canned peaches to the hungry people of the Caucasus.*"

"I haven't seen any macaroni or canned peaches," someone said. "Have you?"

"Perhaps they are on their way," Arnaud said sarcastically.

"*Between the farm lobby in the U.S. and the professional beggars of the Near East, Americans are being subjected to constant appeals for their hard-earned dollars. But nobody is so determined in demanding our help as the Armenians. Every massacre becomes a scheme to get money out of our pockets. Other people around the world kill each other without bothering us about it, but the Armenians imagine that they have a special claim upon our resources, and that when they suffer any injury, it's Americans who must send them biscuits and bandages."*

"That is just perfectly foul."

"How can anyone know what our people here have suffered, and see how desperate the needs are, and yet write something like that?"

"The idealists of the Near East Relief respond to their voice, and experience the self-esteem that comes from do-gooding. In addition, they have the power to make out of a generation of defenseless children whatever they wish. Teaching them in classrooms, providing for them in orphanages, they have a captive audience for their own ideology and beliefs. 'Let us make Armenia in our own image,' they say, and so they do."

Gordon Prior took this as a personal insult. He could only shake his head in dismay.

"We must trust that most people will not read that magazine. Or that they will read it and understand how unfair it is."

"I hope you are not giving them too much credit."

There was a small ruffle of controversy in the United States when the article appeared. But *The Investigator* was not a highly respected publication and its issues could come and go without a great deal of attention. A low current of criticism, however, did pursue the Near East Relief during its entire history, with accusations of "atrocity-mongering" and of exploiting the machinery of charity for some form of profit.

At Kazachi Post, the only tangible consequence of the article was that Ernest Yarrow finally asked Bassgarden to leave. Bundy's accomplice could not be tolerated any longer.

The last they heard, Bassgarden had managed to attach himself to the Toromanian archaeological expedition to the medieval city of Ani.

Built along the Silk Road caravan route, Ani was the capital of the Armenian kingdom in eastern Anatolia in the eleventh century, later abandoned, leaving a site full of interesting ruins. A team of epigraphists, photographers, architects, and other experts was beginning a comprehensive survey of the site, assessing war damage and cataloging what was left.

It was not clear that Bassgarden knew any more about antiquities than he did about livestock. But the man had a remarkable knack for including himself and somehow getting others to support him . . . at least, for a while.

The harvest that summer and fall was far from perfect, but it was the first sign of real success in a very long time. There was enough food to store some for the long winter. They would still need to rely on the N.E.R. food shipments, but it promised better years to come.

Someone learned that turkey was a traditional food in the forests of Georgia. This discovery touched off a burst of planning for something like a proper American-style Thanksgiving feast at the end of November. Penny volunteered to try to work out some pie recipes that could be achieved with their motley collection of ingredients. She asked the boys at Polygon to begin fashioning pie pans from old condensed-milk tins.

But before these plans had advanced very far, Gordon Prior took her aside and asked her to prepare for a trip to Jelal-Oghlu, or rather Stepanavan, with him.

"Penelope dear, I believe we have time for one last trip to the mountains before the winter sets in. After the first of December, they tell me, there will be little traffic over the trails until spring. We have almost finished a set of textbooks for the N.E.R. school up there, and even some extra ones for the government school, at the request of your friend the teacher."

"Oh, I'm so glad you have done that! Thank you! Mr. Chalakyan will be thrilled. Yes, I'm quite willing to go with you."

"The books should be ready by the end of this week. I'll ask Massi Yeretzyan to drive us up there in the mule wagon."

They packed the wagon carefully, as the weight of the books added a degree of challenge. But with only two people in the wagon and their small bit of luggage, there was enough space for them, the books, and a few sacks of grain, onions, and potatoes. They included several blankets and a heavy fur throw, as the late-autumn weather was already brisk and would certainly be colder at the higher elevations.

The day they left, the heavy gray sky and occasional spitting of rain discouraged them a bit. "It's nothing," said Gordon. "It'll be a chilly trip, that's all. We've certainly seen worse. I have promised them these books and I don't want to disappoint them."

But about halfway across the plain to Ghara Kilisa, the rain turned into tiny slivers of ice, and the ground began to crackle underfoot. A hard freeze in November was unusual there, at least in the daytime. Massi Yeretzyan seemed to think that the mules were all right and they should just push on as quickly as possible.

They reached their overnight accommodation at Ghara Kilisa without incident. In the lodging house, everyone wanted to talk about the weather.

Probably they talked mainly about the weather all year long, so that in itself did not mean very much.

In the morning, the stableman informed them that there had been an early snowfall already in the mountains around Stepanavan. He suggested that they hire a sleigh and leave their wagon there to be picked up on their return trip. Massi was dubious, but the man assured him it would be the best course. So, they laboriously transferred their gear into the little sleigh and harnessed the mules to it.

This conveyance was not one of the elegant *troikas* that had carried the former ruling class in style across the frozen steppes of Russia; it was merely a wooden wagon on runners, with a brace extending from each side to keep the clumsy vehicle from tipping over. A proletarian sleigh. But they were assured that it was perfectly sound and that it would be the only safe way to get up to Stepanavan and back.

And they did make it safely to Stepanavan despite the layers of early snow, to Gordon's great satisfaction. The staff members at the barracks orphanage were delighted to see them and to receive the wonderful new books. Grigor Chalakyan came at once to meet them.

"Reverend Prior! Miss Prior! How can we thank you? This means everything to us," cried Grigor. "We have been teaching by recitation and writing with chalk on a wall blackened by charcoal. Not conducive to progress in literacy, I'm afraid."

"We have brought you some pencils but only a little paper—I am sorry," Gordon said. "Paper is so heavy, you know. It was the books or the paper, we couldn't bring both."

"Never mind, we shall manage until God provides."

"It's a pleasure to see you again, Mr. Chalakyan."

"My dear Miss Prior, consider our house your own."

Despite their poverty, the people prepared for them a hot meal of the best they could offer, a chicken stewed in *smetana*, a rich sour cream, full of dark mushrooms harvested from the forest. It was delicious.

"You should not be serving us one of your precious chickens, Mr. Chalakyan."

"Ah, my dear lady, nothing could please us more than to see you enjoy it. But fear not, there is no hen in this dish. It's a fierce and unreliable rooster who got what was coming to him!" They all laughed.

They stayed one more day to allow the mules to rest. Grigor Chalakyan approached them then with another favor to ask.

"I am sure that you want to start your return journey in this interval between bouts of winter weather. Soon, it will be dangerous to make your way through the mountains," he said. "There is a lady here who very much wishes to get back to her husband at the Polygon post. He is a teacher of woodworking there, and she is an orphanage matron who has been helping us for some months. She and her daughter cannot travel alone. So they would like to know if they may accompany you back to Alexandropol."

"You mean Leninakan," Gordon Prior said with a smile. "Yes, of course they may come with us."

"They have their own mule and only a little baggage."

"Really, it's no problem. We will be happy to extend whatever protection we can offer."

"Thank you. They are ready to leave whenever you say."

During the remainder of that day, the temperature dropped dramatically, and it felt very much like winter. They woke the next morning to spatters of crusty white ice forming thick patterns on the rocks around every small trickling stream. The packed snow lay beneath a slick layer of hardened ice. Bare twigs and branches clattered together in a rising wind.

"We'd best get on the road at once," said Gordon. "We surely want to be at Ghara Kilisa before dark."

The lady and her mule were waiting. She introduced herself and her nine-year-old daughter. Gordon urged them to sit inside the sleigh with himself and Penny to be a bit warmer and tie their mule on behind, but she would not hear of it. Instead, the mother and daughter rode their mule and followed the sleigh closely. The mule was an old pack animal that was not accustomed to carrying riders and seemed to think that the whole trip was a bad idea.

The low sky was dark and threatening. A chill mist enveloped them, reducing visibility to nearly nothing. "Wolf weather," grumbled Massi the driver, and Penny remembered why it is that sleighs in the Caucasus were always festooned with bells. Wolves typically used the cover of forest and fog to ambush travelers. But she wondered if the bells would simply attract the wolves like a dinner gong, instead of repelling them.

Thick blasts of snow began to come at their faces, seeming to fall from a height just above the treetops. Now they could barely see what was directly in front of them.

Gordon Prior climbed out of the sleigh and again tried to get the woman and her daughter to sit with them, and again she refused, apparently believing that it was not her place to join them on equal terms . . . an awkward relic of class consciousness. Gordon did tie their mule to the sleigh so that they could keep together in the billows of snow.

They struggled on for miles before Massi had to confess that he had lost the trail. Every gap between the trees looked just like every other. They reached an impasse beyond which the gaps disappeared entirely.

Massi decided that they had to backtrack a bit to a place he could recognize and pick up their trail again. So they retreated, looking for landmarks. All of the mules took a dim view of this enterprise now. Their progress was very slow, and Penny began to worry that they would not be out of the mountains before nightfall.

Eventually they rejoined what Massi thought was the path to Ghara Kilisa.

It was so dark already that one could scarcely distinguish it from night. The path wound around the sides of the mountains, in many places little more than a ledge. They came upon a shelf over a deep crevasse filled with freezing water. It was encrusted with ice, grainy, chunky, white, like frozen milk. At that point, the following mule saw fit to lose its footing on the slippery trail. Its hind end pitched downward and threw its two riders off, directly into the river.

Penny, facing the back of the sleigh, screamed again and again. Gordon turned around and realized what had happened. Throwing off his heavy Near East Relief overcoat, he plunged fully dressed into the water.

He groped around blindly in the inky water, then touched a human being—the little girl. With great effort he lifted her out of the stream and hoisted her onto the bank. Immediately he ducked into the water again, searching for the girl's mother.

Massi managed to pick up the girl and hand her over to Penny. The child was nearly unconscious from shock and exposure. Penny wrapped her tightly in a blanket and sat holding her in the sleigh, trying to warm the little body with her own.

Many long moments passed. Neither Gordon Prior nor the mother resurfaced.

Massi took a lantern from the sleigh and struck a match with shaking hands, finally succeeding in lighting it; he took the lantern and walked up and down the banks of the river, looking for any signs of life. The black freezing water had swallowed them. Its strong current could have taken their bodies anywhere.

The child in Penny's arms was failing; Penny wrapped her in another layer, using Gordon Prior's overcoat, and covered them both with the fur. There was little response. Finally she called out to the driver to come back. "Massi! Massi! We've got to get this girl to shelter. We must move on."

As Penny forced herself to leave that place, she grasped that the child in her arms and she herself had each lost a parent there. Half orphans: one without a mother, one without a father. She gave in to a sobbing, wailing grief.

With difficulty they covered the remaining miles to Ghara Kilisa, reaching it in the middle of the night.

The next day, a search party left at dawn to comb the sides of the river and probe its waters, hoping to find their bodies. They found nothing. They continued to search through the harsh winter and the thawing spring, but both of them were gone.

The news reached Kazachi Post before Penny did.

Jane Eberlee and Arnaud helped to pack up all of their things. She needed to take her father's belongings back to Ohio and reunite with her family there, now also bereaved. Rufus Kendrick, who was nearing the end of his two-year term in Armenia, volunteered to escort her back to her home in Oberlin.

It was hardest to leave her dear girls in the sewing classes. All of them understood grief and loss. Yet they also knew how to survive. "Please don't worry about us, Miss Prior," Mina said. "We know what to do. We will work hard and carry on . . . until you return," she added, with just the very edge of a smile.

Penny wept again when Maritza embraced her and said, "You are truly one of us now." She then whispered in Penny's ear, "Not every story has a happy ending."

The parade ground of the Posts in winter was an open treeless expanse of white in the midst of the low stone barracks built of black volcanic rock, the long slanted roof of each building whited out by snow. All over that open white space moved the figures of children, hundreds at a time, small dark moving objects. If one were to view the scene from above, it would look like the random movement of particles suspended in fluid, like Brownian motion. But each of those objects was a living being, filled with inner warmth and energy, fueled with food, clad in woolen clothing, jackets and britches and skirts and hats, gloves and mittens and stockings and shoes. And each of them was a sign of the victory of love over death.

CHAPTER 9

On the day they were to leave, Penny walked all over Kazachi Post, willing her mind to remember every detail. She stood for a long time in the Saint Arsenius church. And then she forced herself to climb into the boxcar and set her face for the trip to Batoum.

Bibliography

Selected Sources

Anderson, Elizabeth. "Hunting Trouble in Armenia." *Atlantic Monthly* 127/5 (May 1921) 696–707.

Ararat: A Searchlight on Armenia. The Armenian United Association of London. Vol. IV (July 1916–June 1917).

Avakian, Asdghig. *Stranger Among Friends: An Armenian Nurse From Lebanon Tells Her Story.* Beirut: Catholic Press, 1960.

Balakian, Peter. *The Burning Tigris: The Armenian Genocide and America's Response.* New York: HarperCollins, 2003.

Baldwin, Oliver R. *Six Prisons and Two Revolutions: Adventures in Trans-Caucasia and Anatolia, 1920–21.* New York: Doubleday, 1925.

Barrs, Elizabeth Berit. "Marketing the Golden Rule: Near East Relief and Philanthropy's Role in the Political Economy, 1915–1930." M.A. thesis, University of Montana, 2020.

Barton, James L. *Human Progress through Missions.* New York: Fleming H. Revell, 1912.

———. "The Near East Relief: A Moral Force." *International Review of Mission* 18/4 (Oct 1929) 495–502.

Bechhofer, C.E. *In Denikin's Russia and the Caucasus, 1919–1920.* London: W. Collins, 1921.

Burnett, Frances Hodgson. *A Little Princess: Being the Whole Story of Sara Crewe, Now Told for the First Time.* New York: Charles Scribner's Sons, 1905.

Carpenter, Kaley M. "A Worldly Errand: James L. Barton's American Mission to the Near East." Ph.D. dissertation, Princeton Theological Seminary, 2009.

Chater, Melville. "The Land of the Stalking Death: A Journey through Starving Armenia on an American Relief Train." *National Geographic Magazine* 36/5 (Nov 1919) 393–436.

The Cross in the East and the Church in the West. New York: Near East Relief, 1921.

Curti, Merle E. *American Philanthropy Abroad.* New Brunswick, NJ: Transaction Books, 1998.

Daniel, Robert L. *American Philanthropy in the Near East: 1820–1960.* Athens, OH: Ohio University Press, 1970.

Dilworth, Thomas. *David Jones: Engraver, Soldier, Painter, Poet.* Berkeley, CA: Counterpoint, 2017.

Egan, Eleanor Franklin. "This is to be Said for the Turk." *The Saturday Evening Post* 193/25 (20 Dec 1919) 14–15, 71–77.

Earle, Edward Mead. "American Missions in the Near East." *Foreign Affairs* 7/3 (Apr 1929) 398–417.

Eddy, Sherwood. *Everybody's World*. New York: George H. Doran, 1920.

Elder, John. "Memories of the Armenian Republic." *The Armenian Review* 6 (Mar 1953) 3–27.

Elliott, Wendy. *Grit and Grace in a World Gone Mad: Humanitarianism in Talas, Turkey, 1908–1923*. London: Gomidas Institute, 2018.

Farson, Negley. *The Lost World of the Caucasus*. New York: Doubleday, 1958.

Gamble, Richard M. *The War for Righteousness: Progressive Christianity, the Great War, and the Rise of the Messianic Nation*. Wilmington, DE: ISI Books, 2003.

Hall, William H. *The Near East: Crossroads of the World*. New York: Board of Foreign Missions of the Presbyterian Church in the U.S.A., 1920.

Hand Book. New York: Near East Relief, 1920.

Hille, Charlotte. *State Building and Conflict Resolution in the Caucasus*. Eurasian Studies Library series. Leiden: Brill, 2010.

Holmes, Mary Caroline. *Between the Lines in Asia Minor*. Fleming H. Revell, 1923.

Hovannisian, Richard G. *The Republic of Armenia*, vols. 1–4. Berkeley: University of California Press, 1971–1996.

Jackson, Edward. *A Manual of the Diagnosis and Treatment of the Diseases of the Eye*. 2nd ed. Philadelphia: W.B. Saunders, 1907.

Jacobsen, Maria. *Diaries of a Danish Missionary, Harpoot, 1907–1919*. Princeton: Gomidas Institute, 2001.

Johnson, Brian. "Americans Investigating Anatolia: The 1919 Field Notes of Emory Niles and Arthur Sutherland." PDF online. Published in *Journal of Turkish Studies* 34/2 (2010) 129–147.

Karagosian, Arpenia (Araxi Hubbard Dutton Palmer). *Triumph From Tragedy*. Privately printed, 1997.

Laderman, Charlie. *Sharing the Burden: The Armenian Question, Humanitarian Intervention and Anglo-American Visions of Global Order*. Oxford: Oxford University Press, 2019.

Laidlaw, Walter. *The Moral Aims of the War*. New York: Fleming H. Revell, 1918.

Lang, Andrew and Leonora Lang. *The Blue Fairy Book*. Illustrated by H.J. Ford and G.P. Jacomb Hood. New York: Stitt, 1905.

Lapidot-Firilla, Anat. "'Subway Women' and the American Near East Relief in Anatolia, 1919–1924." In *Gendering Religion and Politics: Untangling Modernities*, ed. by H. Herzog and A. Braude, 153–172. Palgrave Macmillan, 2009.

Laycock, Jo. "International Refugee Relief on the Caucasus Front, 1915–16: Perspectives from the Rockefeller Archive Center." RAC Research Reports, 2021.

Lovejoy, Esther Pohl. *Women Physicians and Surgeons: Book Two, Foreign Service*. Livingston, NY: Livingston Press, [1940].

MacDonald, George. *The Princess and the Goblin*. London: Blackie and Son, 1911.

Magee, Malcolm D. *What the World Should Be: Woodrow Wilson and the Crafting of a Faith-Based Foreign Policy*. Waco: Baylor University Press, 2008.

Metaxas, Virginia A. "Dr. Ruth A. Parmelee and the Changing Role of Near East Missionaries in Early Twentieth Century Turkey." In *The Role of the American Board in the World*, ed. by Clifford Putney and Paul T. Burlin, 73–101. Eugene, OR: Wipf & Stock, 2012.

Montgomery, Lucy Maud. *Anne of Green Gables.* Toronto: Ryerson Press, 1908.

Moranian, Suzanne E. "The American Missionaries and the Armenian Question : 1915–1927." Ph.D. diss., University of Wisconsin-Madison, 1994.

A National Test of Brotherhood: America's Opportunity to Relieve Suffering in Armenia, Syria, Persia, and Palestine. American Committee for Armenian and Syrian Relief, 1916.

Nercessian, Nora Nouritza. *The City of Orphans: Relief Workers, Commissars and "Builders of the New Armenia," Alexandropol/Leninakan* 1919–1931. Hollis, NH: Hollis Publishing, 2016.

The New Near East. New York: Near East Relief, 1919–1923.

Ormanian, Malachia. *The Church of Armenia: Her History, Doctrine, Rule, Discipline, Liturgy, Literature and Existing Condition.* 2nd ed., rev. by Terenig Poladian. London: A.R. Mowbray, 1955.

Patenaude, Bertrand M. *The Big Show in Bololand: The American Relief Expedition to Soviet Russia in the Famine of 1921.* Stanford, CA: Stanford University Press, 2002.

Peterson, Merrill D. *Starving Armenians: America and the Armenian Genocide,* 1915–30 *and After.* Charlottesville, VA: University of Virginia Press, 2004.

"The Power of an American Nurse in Lawless Turkey." *The Trained Nurse and Hospital Review* 68/2 (Feb 1922) 114–117.

Richards, George L. *The Medical Work of the Near East Relief: a Review of its Accomplishments in Asia Minor and the Caucasus during* 1919–20. New York: Near East Relief, 1923.

Robinson, Leland Rex. "The Armenian Republic." *The Survey* 43 (3 Jan 1920) 343–347.

Rodogno, Davide. "Beyond Relief: A Sketch of the New East Relief's Humanitarian Operations, 1918–1929." *Monde(s)* 2/6 (2014) 45–64.

Schlesinger, Arthur Jr. "The Missionary Enterprise and Theories of Imperialism." In *The Missionary Enterprise in China and America,* ed. by John K. Fairbank, 336–373. Cambridge, MA: Harvard University Press, 1974.

Scholl, Benjamin Franklin. *Library of Health: Complete Guide to Prevention and Cure of Disease.* Philadelphia: Historical Publishing, 1921.

Swift, Judson. *A Manual of Devotion for Soldiers and Sailors.* New York: American Tract Society, 1918.

They Shall Not Perish: The Story of Near East Relief. Documentary film produced by Shant Mardirossian. Written by George Billard. Yerevan: Acorne, 2017.

Tootikian, Vahan H. *The Armenian Evangelical Church: Yesterday, Today, and Tomorrow.* Southfield, MI: Armenian Heritage Committee, 1996.

Vickrey, Charles V. *Near East Relief: A Review for 1922.* Annual Report to Congress. New York: Near East Relief, 1923.

Watenpaugh, Keith David. *Bread From Stones: The Middle East and the Making of Modern Humanitarianism.* Oakland: University of California Press, 2016.

Wheeler, Mrs. Crosby H. *Missions in Eden: Glimpses of Life in the Valley of the Euphrates.* New York: Fleming H. Revell, 1899.

White, George E. *Adventuring with Anatolia College.* Grinnell, IA: Herald-Register Publishing Company, [1940].

Wigram, William A. *The Cradle of Mankind: Life in Eastern Kurdistan.* 2nd ed. London: A&C Black, 1922.

Winter, J.M. *America and the Armenian Genocide of 1915*. Cambridge: Cambridge University Press, 2003.

Yarrow, Ernest A. "Winter Conditions in the Caucasus." *Journal of International Relations* 11/1 (Jul 1920) 109–119.

Yemelianova, Galina M. and Laurence Broers. *Routledge Handbook of the Caucasus*. London: Routledge, 2020.

Zaroukian, Andranik. *Men Without Childhood*. Trans. by Elise Bayizian and Marzbed Margossian. New York: Ashod Press, 1985.

www.ingramcontent.com/pod-product-compliance
Lightning Source LLC
Chambersburg PA
CBHW060423260626
47161CB00005B/1765